SHADOWED BY AN ANGEL

KATIE-ANNE MARTIN

Shadowed by an Angel
Published by Katie-Anne Martin
New Zealand

© 2017 & 2020 Katie-Anne Martin

ISBN 978-0-473-51213-2 (Softcover)

Production & Typesetting:
Andrew Killick
Castle Publishing Services
www.castlepublishing.co.nz

Cover design:
Initiate Media

Previously published in 2017
by Initiate Media Pty Ltd

This book is dedicated to my treasured friend and fiancé,
Fred Kapera.

CHAPTER ONE

For the purposes of this story which is set in the early nineteen eighties, the spotlight rests upon the small, fictitious town of Shackellby Downes. A sparsely populated region, the town's residents number less than one thousand people. This township is home to a variety of mainly hard-working and friendly folk. As in many small towns, a certain camaraderie exists between the residents, with most knowing each other, at least enough to give a casual greeting in passing. The multiple parks and reserves scattered throughout the region, create many perfect picnic spots, also providing the young people of the community with places for recreation. They can often be seen playing sport, or simply relaxing, chatting on the park benches which are liberally splashed throughout the area.

Stretching the entire length of the farthermost eastern outskirts of the Downes, covering the ground as a blanket, lines of bush-clad ranges provide a picturesque boundary of natural beauty.

Having been largely uninterferred with as yet by the implements of modern man, they also create a safe haven for much wildlife.

Protruding from amongst these bushes is a magnificent mountain, its impressive peak reaching far up into the sky. The steely blue-gray coloured slopes, ever naked, are widely known to be treacherous.

This towering monster stands, a majestic exhibit of nature's grandeur, formidable and silent as a sentinel ever on guard, dwarfing the town at the base of its giant feet.

The townsfolk are, as you would expect, somewhat of a mixed bag.

If asked, most would refer to themselves as being Christians, or at least people who lived their lives by good old-fashioned values. For the most part this was true.

This was a town where people were both generous and hard-working. Incidents of crime in the area were extremely low. Here in the Downes, people did not need to lock the doors to their houses or their vehicles.

On most evenings, the town's three or four hotels were filled with mainly the menfolk who would gather together to enjoy a beer and a game of snooker or darts. The atmosphere in these places was almost always relaxed, and the people accepting of one another, as well as welcoming towards visitors.

The hub of the community was a weatherboard building simply dubbed, the Centre. Having been built mainly by the residents themselves from what had once been little more than a wooden shelter for trampers on the edge of the bushy ranges, after much labour, had been transformed into a house of sorts, containing three large rooms.

The Centre was a place for those who were followers of God, to gather together on a Sunday morning for Church services, which were held under the guidance of the Reverend Mike Brewer and his wife, Christine, who were largely responsible for running the Centre. However, it was also well used throughout the week for a variety of activities, including table tennis games and bingo evenings. The Centre was a general drop-in place to which everyone was welcome.

Coffee and tea were almost always available. On this particular day, over at the Centre, a group of people were gathered in the kitchen, in the throes of peeling vegetables to prepare for a community dinner which was being organized for that evening. As it was a Saturday morning, there were quite a number of people who were available to assist in this task.

Involved in the preparations, was the town's newest resident, nineteen year old Eden McCabe. She had moved from the city to Shackellby Downes only weeks earlier, following the death of her father. Her mother had been taken from the family in a tragic car accident when Eden was just eleven years old. Unfortunately, Eden's father had taken to drinking alcohol in an endeavour to obtain comfort. Eventually, he had become an alcoholic as the liquor took a grip on him. His recent death had been alcohol related as he had contracted cirrhosis of the liver, passing away shortly afterwards. As a result of her father's addiction, Eden had been forced to grow up quickly. Eventually, she had been withdrawn from the private boarding school, where she'd been a pupil, to continue her education locally. This was in order for her to care for her father as he became increasingly unwell. It was left to Eden to attend to the household chores and garden as best she could.

She had been the sole child of her parents and had, at the prompting of her cousin, Vicky Morgan, decided to move to the Downes where Vicky had lived for some time. Eden had shifted in with her cousin to share the modern two bed-roomed unit which was tenanted by Vicky. The cousins had maintained a strong bond, having kept in touch regularly, even though they had seen very little of each other during the previous ten or so years. Both girls were followers of God, with Eden being just recently so. Eden was, at five feet nine inches in stockinged feet, tall for a woman, with a slim figure which accentuated her height. Her long, shining hair was dark in colour with a mass of curls which cascaded down her back. Eden's eyes, however, were her most noticeable feature.

Hazel in colour, they sparkled with enthusiasm and intelligence, as well as the God-given love and joy she had recently come to know. From the first, many of the locals had been drawn to this young woman with her vibrant personality and caring nature which attracted them.

It had taken very little time for Eden to be widely accepted by almost everyone in the small township. As a result, she had made friends quickly with many people.

Eden's cousin, Vicky, was, in contrast to Eden, fair headed. She often wore her straight, sandy coloured hair tied up in a pony tail at the back of her head. At five feet five inches in height, Vicky was also shorter than Eden. However, the cousins were both fine boned and slender in build. Vicky, now aged twenty one years, had been a wilful and 'hot-headed' teenager. She was, to this day, not close to the members of her immediate family. Having left home at just seventeen years of age, she had completed a course in office work before travelling overseas for a short time. Vicky had finally settled for small town life, joining the close-knit community in the Downes, where she was now employed as a teller in one of the local banks. Since becoming a Christian, she had softened considerably in her manner, which came also with maturity. However, she remained a person with strongly held opinions on a variety of issues. Some of these she clung to stubbornly, voicing her rigid views a little inappropriately at times. Even though Vicky presented as quite a closed-minded young lady, her fellow residents, for the most part, cared for her deeply, realizing that she possessed a kind heart as well as being, generally, a well-intentioned person. That morning Vicky was also assisting with the kitchen duties at the Centre. She was showing signs of slacking in her work, as there was a huge amount of vegetables still to be prepared. Edith Hunt, a lady who was also involved, noticing that Vicky was becoming a little irritable, spoke to her in an attempt to spur the young woman on.

"Come on, Vicky," she said encouragingly, "we are at least halfway through, and remember that we are doing this for a good cause."

She then added jokingly, "Just another three thousand potatoes to peel and we'll be finished." Armed with an extra long carrot, Vicky advanced towards her, then burst into laughter. Sighing, she picked up the peeler she had discarded and replied somewhat unenthusiastically, "Yes, I guess so. I just didn't realize how long this would take."

Eden laughed and spoke to her cousin, "This is good training for when you get married and have six children."

In reply, Vicky grimaced.

She stated, as she had many times, that marriage and a family were not in her life plans. All who were gathered, laughed, as they knew that Vicky was a 'tomboy' who had no intention of ever settling for family life – at least not in the near future. It was a standing joke among those who knew her well and Vicky was forever being teased about her stance on the matter.

Reverend Mike Brewer was the minister at the Centre. He, along with his wife, Christine, and their two high school aged boys, Allan and Drew, had moved to the area to take up this position approximately five years ago. The Brewer family had become widely respected among their fellow residents, including those who shunned church meetings, as many times, the couple had shown their love of the locals in various practical ways. These included the cooking of meals for people, as well as lending a helping hand in general to those who needed it – be it the boarding up of a broken window, or the mowing of a lawn for those who were elderly or infirm. Mike and Christine would also encourage people who lived alone, as well as some of the more lonely residents, to join in with the huge variety of activities that were held at the Centre on a regular basis. Many a night, they invited folks for dinner at their modest home.

Mike was a tall, heavily set, yet gentle bear of a man, with a shock of curly, light brown hair, which seemed to sit on the top of his head. His wife, Christine, was fair headed and small in stature.

She was a softly spoken lady and a woman who possessed much wisdom. Christine was also a caring and attentive listener.

Consequently, many people would seek her out to discuss their various problems. All found her to be compassionate, as well as genuinely loving, towards those with whom she came into contact.

A young man named Mark Hanson was also heavily involved in helping to organize many of the activities that were held in the Centre. At twenty two years of age, he was just over six feet in height. His mousey, collar-length hair was slightly wavy. Mark had brown eyes which seemed to always shine, reflecting his enthusiasm for life and effervescent personality.

He was a young man who, indeed, squeezed as much out of life as he was able to, living his life to the full. Although dedicated to his job, Mark also filled his leisure time to overflowing with many and varied activities. He was an electrician by trade, and, as a result, his skills came in handy when problems arose at the Centre that required the attention of someone with his expertise. He was many times called upon to provide assistance, which he was more than willing to freely give as required.

Like most members of the Centre, he also cared for people. Mark was very much a person through whom the love of his God shone, drawing many into friendship with him. As the workers were toiling, he popped into the Centre, in search of Mike Brewer. Immediately, Vicky threw a potato peeler at him which he awkwardly caught. Quickly assessing the situation, Mark joined in the fun. Playfully, he looked at the peeler and jokingly asked, "What on earth is this? I must say that I have never seen one of these strange looking items before in my life."

Everyone erupted into laughter, as he turned it this way and that, as if it were a foreign object to him.

"Come on," Vicky insisted, "even a man is able to do something as simple as peel vegetables."

Mark laughed and quickly exited the room, looking over his shoulder on his way out to apologize with a huge grin, saying, "Sorry I can't help, although I'd love to, of course, but important business calls."

Vicky groaned dramatically as he left the Centre, and jumped into his car. She then said to her fellow work mates, "Now that's just one reason among many as to why I never want to marry."

Edith grinned and replied that her husband had learned to do house-hold chores early on in their marriage.

"It was either he learn how to assist with the meal preparations or remain unfed," she joked.

Vicky chuckled, then asked, "Wasn't it a man that first said that a woman's place was in the kitchen anyway?"

As the friendly chatter continued, time passed quickly, and finally, to the relief of all, the hard work was finished, and preparations for the evening's meal complete. As a single man, Mark had been quick to notice Eden McCabe. He was drawn to her warm, caring personality, as well as finding her physically attractive. He spoke to Mathew Hall, a close friend about this, telling him of his desire to get to know her a little better, as well as asking his opinion. Mathew replied that Eden was indeed attractive and seemed to be a young woman with a lovely nature.

Mark confessed to his friend. "I feel a little shy for some reason, and unsure of just how to approach her."

Mathew laughed and replied, "That's not like you, mate. You don't have a shy bone in your body."

Mark smiled and told his friend that although he and Eden knew each other slightly, their contact, to this point, had been limited and had always been in a group setting.

Mathew advised Mark to simply be himself. "You will be fine," he said encouragingly, then jokingly asked his friend how on earth any female could resist him. The two men laughed, then enjoyed a time of lighthearted banter before parting company.

The following Sunday, after church at the Centre, Mark approached Eden and asked her if she would like to accompany him to a cafe for coffee some time. Eden enthusiastically agreed, saying that she would enjoy that, and the two chatted for a short while, mostly about the morning's sermon at church which had been about spending quality time with God.

Both agreed that Mike Brewer had delivered an excellent message. Finally, Eden excused herself, explaining to Mark that she had been invited to lunch that day by Dorothy Moore, who, by the looks of it, was now ready to leave. Quickly scribbling her contact details down on a piece of paper, Eden handed them to Mark and they said their goodbyes.

...

The community dinner that evening turned out to be a roaring success, with all in attendance enjoying the evening. The meal was first class as well. One hundred and forty potatoes had been peeled and cooked, as well as about two hundred carrots, along with other vegetables. Chicken, beef, and a selection of cold meats were among other items served. After dinner, people gathered around the piano which was played by Dorothy Moore, who played a selection of golden oldies, which many sang along to with enthusiasm.

The people then sat down to participate in a lighthearted game of bingo, with lollipops as prizes.

Mike Brewer called the numbers and, with his humour, soon had the crowd laughing uproariously.

The evening was brought to an end with the serving of tea and coffee for those who wanted it, along with several plates of Dorothy Moore's home-made blueberry muffins. This was the kind of simple fun enjoyed by the whole community on a regular basis, with many participating in the various activities held in the township. Having weathered their fair share of storms as a community, the locals always 'looked out' for one another, being quick to assist those who were going through difficult times. In fact, were this town to have a motto, I believe it would have read something like this:

Arm in Arm We Stand – Together We Overcome.

CHAPTER TWO

The town's central shopping area was laid out in the shape of a large rectangle, with fifty or more shops and businesses stretching side by side, around the entire outer edge of the two blocks it encompassed.

Putting to good use the space inside this elongated square of commercial outlets, a large mall had been created. This mall was accessible both day as well as at night via a small alley way which was sandwiched between a toy store and a bakery. Wooden benches and tables had been liberally placed around the area, and a selection of native trees, as well as huge pot plants, provided both scenic beauty as well as a little shelter for people when needed. This entire area was paved with old-fashioned cobblestones. Many of the town's workers would gather together regularly to enjoy their lunchtime breaks in these pleasant surroundings. Others, taking a rest from their shopping, would simply sit and relax for a while. This mall was a popular place for residents, who were often seen congregating together in small groups to chat, or just to sit quietly alone when they so desired.

At this time, Eden and her cousin, Vicky Morgan, were sitting together, as they reflected on years passed. Vicky complimented her cousin, telling her how well she looked. In reply, Eden smiled a little, thanking Vicky for the compliment. She then went on to say that she had endured some tumultuous years since the passing of her mother.

"It was difficult," Eden spoke softly, "growing up without mum around. Especially during my teenage years. I was no longer attending the school that I loved and, as a result, lost touch with most of my friends."

Vicky looked quietly at Eden for a time before replying.

"I guess that, compared to you, my life was pretty stable," she finally said. "Although I did not appreciate my family, they raised me as best they knew how."

The cousins were quiet for a moment, each engrossed in their individual thoughts. Then Eden spoke again, as tears filled her eyes. "The very hardest part was having to watch my dad slipping into alcoholism. It swamped him, and being so young myself with almost no support, I felt helpless.

"Finally, as his drinking became worse, it was left to me to care for him, to cook and to clean, and during the last months of his life, I became like a full time caregiver to him." She continued, "I grew to be quite angry having to pour such a large amount of my life into looking after him. It didn't seem fair. He became completely self-centred, and only interested in having his meals and basic needs met, and, of course, the alcohol that he was never without. I was the loser," Eden said, "giving up my adolescent years because I felt obliged to care for him. During those years, I yearned to be like other girls my age – to attend dances and enjoy movies. I really did feel so cut off and isolated."

Vicky gently squeezed her cousin's hand. "I am so sorry for all that you endured," she replied. "And also sorry that I was doing my rebellious 'thing' and was not there to support you."

Eden managed a wan smile, and then, in almost a whisper, confessed to Vicky that during those years, she had regularly starved herself, at times also regurgitating her food, in an effort to obtain some kind of control in a life that had completely and unfairly begun to overwhelm her. Shocked to hear this, Vicky glanced quickly at her cousin's slim figure and asked her if she still did this to herself.

Eden tossed her head slightly, as if to distance herself from the question, before answering, "Sometimes."

Vicky said in reply, "I have always known you to be a confident and secure person. You certainly hide your insecurities well."

Eden answered her cousin, "To cover up well, takes practice and lots of it. Paying attention to my personal appearance assists me to feel more confident," she continued. "It is important to me that I dress well and look my best. I guess that I am a bit of a perfectionist in that area," she admitted. "But knowing that I look good, carries me a long way. Belonging to God, and knowing that He loves me, also helps," she added.

Vicky gently said to Eden, "Thank you for trusting me enough to share these things with me." Eden smiled, and then requested that Vicky keep all that she had said in the strictest of confidence.

"Of course," Vicky responded. The two young women sat in silence again. Finally, Eden once again spoke saying, "I am glad to be here with you now, beginning a new life."

Vicky nodded in agreement, "Me, also," she said.

The two girls finally got to their feet and slowly walked home with neither one speaking.

That evening, while Vicky watched some television in the unit they now shared, Eden walked into her bedroom and closed the door. She opened a drawer in her dressing table, and pulled out a framed photo of both her mother and father which had been taken in happier times. Sitting on her bed, the young woman quietly wept. She longed to be able to recapture that long lost stability she had once enjoyed.

Then, after carefully replacing the photograph in between some clothes in her drawer, she lay on her bed deep in thought as a feeling of an intense sorrow overwhelmed her.

Included in the central shopping area were two florist stores, one of which Eden had managed to secure employment in. She had enjoyed arranging flowers for as long as she could remember, as her mother had planted well kept rows of a variety of flowers, which had run the length of the family property. She had taught Eden at a young age, how to tend the flowers. She also passed on to the young girl, her expertise at arranging them. Carnations, in particular, were among Eden's favourites, as she fondly remembered her mother's particular love of them.

A few coffee shops, as well as several clothes stores, four large supermarkets, and a well used post office, made up just a few of the available shops for the purchasing needs of the townsfolk. There were, of course, many other shopping choices, a surprisingly large selection for such a small town. Approximately two miles to the left of the town's centre, on the corner of Muirley and Atticca Streets, was a small schoolyard, containing nine classrooms in total. This school serviced all of the town's Intermediate and High School aged youth. Thirteen staff were employed at the school complex. The children of primary school age attended a separate school which was a little closer to town. This school was situated on a street named Walker Terrace. With a roll of just fifty-five pupils, only four teachers were employed here, with one of them doubling as Head Mistress.

For the most part, the youth of the Downes enjoyed school. Pupils at both schools were a bit like family, as being so few in number, they were close knit youngsters. They tended to look out for one another as, out of the school setting, many of their families knew one another. As a result, apart from the odd incident, the children mixed together well. Teaching standards were high for such a small community.

Consequently, by the time the older students were ready to leave school, in many cases to continue their education out of town, they had been well prepared for this. The town was equipped, also, with six or so doctors, all of whom were general practitioners, as well as a medical centre/mini hospital, which was equipped with two beds available to be used for a variety of mainly minor problems. People with serious medical needs were sent to the nearest city to be cared for. The entire township was serviced by a total of four ambulances and, as most residents would agree, an inadequate amount of fire and police services.

Meanwhile, in one of the town's cafes, Dorothy Moore and Christine Brewer were conversing over a cup of coffee. The two friends were discussing ways in which the Centre could be utilized more fully by locals. Dorothy suggested that a supervised dance on a fortnightly, or even weekly basis for the younger members of the community, might be an idea with merit.

"This would give the teenagers an added activity in which to engage," she explained to Christine, who nodded in approval. "We could even ask one or two of the ladies if they would be willing to hold dance classes if there was enough interest," she commented.

Dorothy laughed, saying that when she was a teenager, everyone was forced to learn how to dance properly. "I don't mean the disco style of today's youth," she said, "but the more formal type of dancing, which I personally believe that everyone should be taught how to do at least reasonably well."

She continued to speak. "It's good preparation for the youngsters for later in their lives."

Christine agreed, and asked Dorothy if she would be willing to look into the possibility.

"I would be happy to," Dorothy told her friend. "Leave it with me."

The two women chatted for a while longer, each enjoying the company of the other. Then Dorothy asked after Christine's family. Christine gave a small sigh before replying. "Mike is working as hard as ever," she said. "I honestly don't think that he knows how to slow down and to just take it easy." She continued. "Both boys have come down with some kind of tummy bug and are off school right now," she said.

Dorothy reached over and touched her friend's shoulder, promising to keep the family in her prayers, and the two then sat for a few minutes, in a comfortable silence.

Christine then asked Dorothy how life was for her, to which Dorothy replied, "A bit lonely at times but I can't really complain," she smiled. Dorothy was a short, plumpish woman aged fifty-nine years, with a mass of white curly hair which she kept neatly trimmed. She had lost her husband only four years previous as the result of a freak building accident. The couple had been married for only ten years.

Having married later in life, they had not raised a family, and to this day, Dorothy missed him dreadfully. She told Christine that she was enjoying getting to know young Eden McCabe. "It's lovely to sit and just listen to her chat," she said. "In fact, she is starting to become very much like a daughter to me."

In response to this, Christine smiled and replied, "Eden's enthusiasm for God, as well as for life in general, is certainly very refreshing."

Finally, Dorothy got to her feet, explaining to Christine that she needed to get home in order to prepare for some visitors whom she was expecting later in the day.

The friends said their goodbyes and, after having made another time to meet together, went their separate ways.

In the central shopping area today, as on many occasions, the unmistakable shrill voice of Veronica Hartley could be heard before she was sighted. A hefty lady in her mid forties, with a large bosom, gaudy make-up, and brightly coloured red hair worn in a tight perm, she was an extremely colourful character. Veronica's clothing was always bright, also, as she tottered about in high heeled shoes that seemed to be a size too small for her.

Veronica was widely known as the town 'gossip' and was avoided whenever possible by most of her fellow residents. This time, she had managed to bail up one of the local women, to whom she was loudly voicing her disapproval of the fact that the seventeen year old daughter of one of the town's council members, was now living with her boyfriend.

Veronica's penetrating voice reached fever pitch as she became increasingly dramatic.

"I tell you," she said in no uncertain terms, "that man should be ashamed of himself. Fancy allowing his daughter to live in this way, outside of marriage. I tell you," she repeated, barely pausing for breath, "when I was young, situations like this were unheard of."

Veronica then lowered her voice to that of a stage whisper as she delivered her verbal finale. "If you ask me, she's nothing more than a tramp."

Her reluctant audience squirmed before somehow managing to extract herself from Veronica's company. She fled gratefully from Veronica's vocal soliloquy which continued on, as if this loud-mouthed woman was unaware that she had lost her audience.

Meeting with silence, she pursed her thin lips and walked off shaking her head in disgust. As she tottered down the road, her beady eyes scanned the street, seeking another victim to express her views on the matter to.

Married to Bob Hartley, Veronica would often complain about her husband's hearing difficulties.

"He is getting worse," she would rant. "These days he cannot seem to hear a word I say. It's so difficult to live with a husband who is deaf," she would moan.

However, it seemed that, in fact, Bob was able to hear quite clearly when in the company of his friends and work mates during evenings at the local hotel. He was the object of sympathy to many, all of whom wondered how he could have remained married to his talkative and often sharp-tongued wife for more than twenty years. Veronica was disliked by most of the townsfolk, although she was always good for an update on the latest scandals and happenings around town. Her gossip was exaggerated and flavoured with her own views on whatever she was speaking about. She seemed to particularly thrive on the misfortunes of others, using them as an excuse to voice her opinions as well as to exercise her over-active vocal chords.

In the main, she was ignored by most, with her hapless husband being dubbed a saint of sorts by his friends, all of whom realized that his so-called hearing problems were completely selective, being merely a coping mechanism for the times he spent at home in the company of his loud and intrusive wife.

Also in town that day, Bob Fulton, the town's mayor, walked quickly along the street with his deputy in tow. Bob was short in stature, with sharp features. He was the kind of man who never seemed to quite look you in the eye. He was a rapid thinker and generally spoke quickly as well. Morrie Whetton, his overweight deputy, was heavily perspiring as he struggled to match strides with the fast-paced Mr Fulton. The two men were involved in some kind of muted discussion as they strode along Ashville Street, finally turning left into Woodley Avenue.

Dorothy Moore walked briskly along Ashville Street, the town's main street, on her way home. She lived in a two roomed cottage on Hallevale Avenue on the outskirts of the town. Although she owned a vehicle, she often preferred to travel on foot. At the back of her large section was a small self-contained flat which had been unoccupied for some years now. Her nephew, Johnathon, had been the last person to dwell in the flat, having passed away almost eight years ago while living in the unit.

Dorothy liked to keep busy, and was active in her community, as well as being a valued member of the Centre. In fact, she possessed the distinction of being one of the Centre's first members.

She was a softly spoken woman, as well as a devoted follower of God. Dorothy dedicated much time to prayer, and was also a lady who refused to listen to, or indulge in, gossip. A woman of her word, she was trusted by many of her fellow residents, most of whom respected and loved her.

Her faith in God was reflected beautifully in the way that she lived her life.

Although not a wealthy woman, Dorothy gave freely of what she possessed to those in need.

She was kindly, yet wise, and despised hypocrisy. She frowned upon it in others, as well as being careful to keep it far from her own life. She was a gifted pianist, enjoying many a night with people who would gather around the piano, as she played a wide variety of songs for folk to sing along to. The love she showed towards others was unfeigned, and she would often invite people to visit her at her cottage for a meal, or simply a chat over coffee and biscuits.

Eventually, when Mark had summoned up the courage to phone Eden, the two met for coffee.

However, they both felt a little ill at ease and each was disappointed at how the morning turned out.

It had been punctuated with awkward moments, as Eden, alone with Mark, somehow lacked the confidence she enjoyed when engaging with him in a group setting.

Mark, in turn, was nervous, and stumbled over his words a number of times. The two parted, with each having made up their minds to take the time to truly get to know one another before attempting an outing of this type again – if, in fact, it was ever to happen again in the future.

The relationship between Dorothy and Eden was becoming an increasingly close one. The younger woman had begun to confide in, as well as to seek guidance from Dorothy, as, over time, the two formed a deep and special bond.

Eden had become a regular visitor to Dorothy's small cottage, and the two women spent much time chatting, or simply relaxing in Dorothy's living room. Eden found Dorothy to be a caring and attentive listener, and was able to share with the older woman, many of her deepest insecurities and fears. Eventually, she came to find in Dorothy, the mother figure she had so desperately longed for ever since her own mother had been tragically taken from her.

CHAPTER THREE

Eden enjoyed the company of the many friends whom she had quickly made in the township.

Some of these were also friends of Mark Hansen. As a group, they would regularly meet for coffee or a meal. Sometimes, they would see a movie together at the local cinema. All of these people had been welcoming towards Eden, and quick to involve her in their activities.

She gradually developed a close friendship with Mark Hansen as she got to know him better.

His kind and gentle nature caught her attention. As well as that, she liked his sense of humour – which was not unlike her own. As their friendship grew, they discovered that they had much in common. Both enjoyed travelling, and they also shared an irrepressible enthusiasm for life as well as a deep devotion to their God.

Eden found Mark to be a good listener and Mark, in turn, would often sit enthralled as Eden chatted away to him. One evening, as Mark and Eden were sitting alone on the steps outside the Centre, Mark asked Eden what she was planning to do to celebrate her twentieth birthday which was approaching. "I don't know," she replied. "Have you any ideas?"

Mark's reply was immediate. "Yes," he said. "I could whip you away to a desert island and we could feast on sun-baked snails," he suggested lightheartedly.

Eden laughed, then suggested that a tropical island might be a little more suitable.

Mark and Eden had, by now, begun to spend an increasing amount of time together, especially so over the last few months. In fact, of recent times, Mark had begun taking Eden out alone on dates. They laughed and chatted over restaurant meals, as well as 'deluxe' picnics. They were becoming quite fond of each other, and this increased as they spent more time together. Eden found Mark to be excellent company. He was intelligent as well as fun to be around. Just lately, some would say that there seemed to be an extra sparkle in Eden's bright hazel-coloured eyes whenever she was around Mark.

It was about this time that Mark began to spend extra time in prayer, seeking guidance from his God concerning one particular area of his life. After a few weeks, he felt that he had received his answer. He then asked Eden to do likewise, requesting that she go to God in prayer also, which she did.

After a few weeks had passed, they met to talk, comparing notes on what each had felt that the Lord was showing them. They spoke intensely, for quite a length of time, before parting company.

As Mark walked Eden to her car, he leaned over, and, for the first time ever, kissed her gently on the cheek. In reply,

Eden smiled, glowing radiantly, before they each drove off in their separate vehicles.

The following day during the lunch hour, there was a meeting being held at the Centre for all members. They were gathering to discuss the ins and outs of a concert being organized by the group for the residents of the Downes. Many of the members of the Centre were talented people, possessing a wide variety of gifts. Mark was an excellent guitarist, while several other members were able to sing beautifully. One of the men was an expert at juggling, being able to juggle six table tennis balls successfully at one time.

Hugh Muirhead was a 34 year old, intellectually handicapped man who played the mouth organ with excellence. As well as that, Mike Brewer was a particularly talented stand-up comic and Dorothy Moore played the piano well.

This particular morning, both Eden and Mark were unable to attend this meeting as each of them had business to attend to. Dorothy gave their apologies to the assembled group. The following week, at a second meeting to further discuss and plan the concert, both Eden and Mark were in attendance. Mark explained to the group that he had thought of an original idea for an extra special closing act for the event. A grand finale with a difference.

After sharing his idea with those present, everyone showed enthusiasm, agreeing that it was an absolutely perfect and unique closing act. Following more discussion concerning the various items to be included in the evening's entertainment, a date was set for the concert to be held, and a venue selected. All in attendance were cautioned to remain silent about the concert's closing act so that it would remain a surprise for locals on the night of the event.

Everyone in the room was excited, agreeing to keep this special finale to the concert a secret, although this would be difficult for some of the Centre's members. The meeting ended with the compiling of a list of the various performances that would make up the evening's entertainment. As well as that, a timetable for practice sessions was drawn up and handed out to those who were to be involved.

Then, business having been completed, coffee and tea were served for all, along with a plate of Dorothy Moore's home-made strawberry muffins.

Mark had requested that Eden be involved in the concert's finale. She readily agreed.

Everyone present was certain that an act such as this would 'bring the house down'.

The impending concert was publicized, and the residents became excited, as many had attended previous events of this kind put on by members of the Centre. They had found them to be of high quality, as well as excellent entertainment. Although the townsfolk knew nothing of what they were to expect at this particular event, rumours had somehow spread that there was to be a special item to close the show.

Interest was heightened, as many of the residents wondered what this special performance would entail. Some thought that a guest artist from out of town might be brought in to make an appearance. However, no-one was sure of what the organizers had planned. As you can imagine, when the evening of the concert arrived, there was an unusually high turnout among the townsfolk.

As people scrambled for seats in the large town hall, the performers were engaged back stage in last minute preparations.

Finally, with the opening of the curtains, the entertainment began. A small choir had prepared a medley of songs which was delivered beautifully by the talented singers, accompanied by Dorothy Moore on the piano. Among the acts to follow, was a short play in which both Eden and Mark participated. Mark played the part of a prince while Eden made a lovely-looking princess.

The plot was simple, yet very entertaining. Of course, Mike Brewer's comedy act was a hit, as was the mouth organ recital. Every performance was of a high standard, being thoroughly enjoyed by the audience.

The stage curtains closed for the final time without anything too extraordinary seeming to have taken place. Seconds later, as if on cue, Vicky Morgan, seated among the crowd, called for an encore. In response to this, the stage curtains opened once more to reveal all of the concert's participants standing on stage. As a group, they took a bow and the audience clapped, cheering loudly. The curtains were once again closed. However, no-one in the audience moved from their seats. There seemed to be a kind of shuffling sound coming from behind the curtains, and they were shortly opened again. Only Mark and Eden were on stage this time, standing, facing each other, still dressed in their prince and princess costumes. The crowd leaned forward, anticipating a comedy act of some kind, as Eden and Mark had teamed up before as comics, with much success. Those gathered realized that this must be the 'grand finale,' and wondered what was to come. To the amazement of all, except a few people who had been sworn to secrecy, Mark Hansen, getting down on one knee in front of a blushing Eden, asked her if she would be his princess forever.

A radiant Eden shyly responded with a resounding, "Yes!" and the crowd watched in complete silence as Mark slipped a delicate ring on to Eden's slim finger.

For a moment, there was confusion amongst those watching, as they wondered if this was truly a marriage proposal, or merely the beginning of another skit.

Mark, moving to the front of the stage, addressed the audience. "This is not an act," he stated. "I have indeed asked Eden to marry me and this beautiful lady at my side has agreed to be my bride." He continued speaking as the crowd sat enthralled. "I wish to tell you all that Eden and I are now officially engaged to be married. Actually," he confessed, "Eden agreed to be my wife two weeks ago, but we decided to announce it tonight, as many of you are special to us both."

He then turned and embraced his fiancée, as the audience, roaring with approval, stood to their feet. It was agreed by all in attendance that the concert had been a tremendous success, with the surprise announcement a wonderful highlight. In fact, it was spoken of fondly by locals for quite some time. This had been an evening which many would not forget.

CHAPTER FOUR

Although Eden and Mark's wedding date was only six months away, the nuptials were not quite the next big occasion on Eden's calendar. She had been planning for some time now to attend a school reunion which was to be held at Neptune Middle School – the school she had attended during her intermediate school years. This school building, even now still used to teach in, was approximately three and a half day's journey by car from the Downes. Now only one week away, it was time for Eden to organize herself for the trip. She was excited at the prospect of renewing friendships – many of which had been close while she was at school, although contact had long since been lost with even the closest of her friends over time.

She planned to break her journey by spending each night at a reasonably priced back-packers' hostel, or bed and breakfast house, which she had decided not to prebook, as there were many of these places dotted along the road she was to travel. Although she would miss Mark terribly, the reunion was to be held for one week only, and she was looking forward to it immensely.

"I will phone you at every opportunity," she tearfully promised Mark as she kissed him tenderly, ruffling his hair fondly, before she left.

"I will miss you as well, sweetheart," Mark responded as the couple embraced.

Then, sliding behind the wheel of her small vehicle, Eden wound down the car window to once more wrap her arms around the 'love of her life.'

After again kissing Mark, she drove off while he stood waving until she had rounded a corner and disappeared from sight.

"Dear God," he prayed, "keep her safe on the roads and bring her safely home. Thank you so much for bringing Eden into my life, Lord," he whispered.

Meanwhile, Eden drove from the Downes via the north-bound motorway, and was soon well into her journey. She had also prayed for Mark's safety, and she drove in silence for some time before turning on the car's radio for some company.

Mark walked slowly back into the villa he owned in the Downes. He was already missing Eden and looking ahead to the day she was to return. Then, smiling, he turned his electric jug on in order to make himself a mid-morning cup of coffee, which he decided to sip on while reading the local daily newspaper. A week seemed to him, at that moment, a very long time for Eden to be away. "I guess it will pass quickly," he reassured himself. Then, picking up the newspaper, he sat in an easy chair to enjoy his drink.

That evening, after having received the promised phone call from Eden, Mark decided to visit with friends, which eventually turned into an evening of playing board games which they all enjoyed.

After a refreshing sleep that night, Mark awoke early for work the following day. Now and then throughout the day, his thoughts drifted to Eden whom he hoped wasn't becoming weary with all of the travelling she was needing to do.

That evening after dinner, Eden had not yet phoned, so to fill in some time while he waited, Mark played a few games of solitaire. By 8.30, however, having still not received a call from her, he decided to visit a friend for coffee, assuming that she had probably been unable to access a telephone.

The following morning was a Wednesday and Mark, feeling a little low because he had not been able to speak with 'his girl', went off to work. However, by the end of that evening, when Eden had once again failed to make contact, Mark became a little anxious. "Why had she not been able to call him?" he wondered. He then prayed fervently for Eden's safety before retiring to bed for the night.

He was slightly worried, although he did his best to reassure himself. "She will be all right," he reasoned.

Surely she would call the following day when she had arrived at the reunion gathering.

Again, Mark slept fairly well.

However, there was no phone contact from Eden the next day, or the day after. By now Mark, as well as others of Eden's friends, was becoming concerned.

Before leaving town, Eden had mentioned her intentions to call on one of her and Mark's mutual friends for a catch up, while on her journey. This friend lived in a small town she was to pass through on her way to her destination. After some time, Mark found the telephone number of this lady and phoned her. Although slightly relieved after talking to this person, to have been reassured that Eden had, indeed, visited with her and had been in good spirits, Mark was aware that this did not explain Eden's failure to contact him. Over the following forty-eight hours, he spoke to Christine and Mike Brewer, seeking their advice as to what he should do. Mike told him to give it another day or so, as Eden was probably too busy enjoying catching up with old friends to think about phoning home. Mark took his pastor's advice, although reluctantly so. He felt that this lack of contact from Eden, was out of character for the young woman, whom he knew loved him dearly. He knew that she was not the type of person to get so involved in what she was doing, that she would fail to phone her new fiancé, especially as she knew that he was awaiting her calls.

By the fifth day, without any contact from Eden, Mark decided to phone the Neptune School building, as, by this time, he had become fearful that something had happened to his sweetheart.

He thought that if he could just ascertain that she was safely at the reunion, his mind would be eased. He might even get to speak with her. After a few problems obtaining the telephone number, Mark called the school. After a brief conversation, however, he thumped the telephone back into its cradle, as he broke into a cold sweat. Panicking at what he had been told on the phone, he quickly jumped into his car, and headed for Dorothy Moore's home. Upon his arrival at her cottage, Mark banged loudly on the front door which was quickly opened by Dorothy. She ushered him inside.

She, in turn, became distressed by what her young visitor had to say to her.

Upon phoning the school, Mark explained he had been informed that Eden, in fact, had not arrived at her destination to register for the reunion, as had been expected. The organizers of the large event had simply concluded that she had decided not to attend after all, for some reason. By now, Mark knew that something was dreadfully wrong. What had happened to Eden?

CHAPTER FIVE

Mark sat at Dorothy's kitchen table in a state of shock. "We need to call the police," he stated without moving.

"Of course," Dorothy replied, upset herself, although trying to be positive. She spoke to Mark. "You realize that Eden's car may have broken down somewhere along the way."

However, her words were spoken with little conviction.

"She would have contacted me," Mark replied in a monotone.

"Yes, I guess she would have," Dorothy conceded, then briefly touching the young man's trembling shoulders, she stood to her feet.

"Leave the phone call to me," she told Mark, who was by this time wracked with sobs.

He nodded in response, as Dorothy called the local police station.

After speaking with an officer, she informed Mark that a policeman was shortly to visit them to gather some information. She suggested that it would be a good idea to call Mike and Christine Brewer, as well as Eden's cousin, Vicky, so that they could be present when the policeman arrived. Mark did not respond, so Dorothy phoned the various people, all of whom immediately drove to her home. Dorothy then quickly dialed the telephone number to the reunion's venue, asking for directions to the school from Shackellby Downes. As it happened, there were several routes that Eden could have taken. With no idea of which road she had travelled, they all agreed to stay put until they had spoken with the police.

After about twenty minutes or so, a sharp knock on Dorothy's front door signalled the arrival of the constable who wrote down Eden's description and other relevant details. He endeavoured to reassure her friends and fiancé, although conceding that it seemed that the young woman had indeed gone missing. After taking statements from those gathered, the police officer promised to be in touch, explaining to them that he would contact a larger police station in the city to assist in trying to locate Eden.

Suddenly, Mark leaped to his feet and spoke, his voice hoarse with emotion. "I am going to find her – she can't have just disappeared."

Before anyone was able to stop him, he had jumped into his vehicle and, taking off with a squeal of tyres, he sped down Dorothy's driveway and out onto the road. Mike and Christine quickly got into their car to follow him, as they feared that in his panic and shocked state, it was possible that he would put himself, or someone else on the roads, in danger. Dorothy and Vicky stayed by the telephone as Dorothy put the kettle on to make coffee.

They all felt useless, as it seemed that there was little that could be done except to wait for the police to investigate, and, of course, to pray, which Vicky and Dorothy now did fervently.

As Mark sped along the motorway, heading out of town, he looked about him for any sign of Eden's car or of Eden herself. However, his efforts were fruitless. Fortunately, he didn't get far as his driving was erratic and, as a consequence, was soon stopped by a traffic officer who, after a short struggle, removed Mark's car keys from him, escorting him back to Dorothy's home.

Firmly, he told Mark to leave the search for Eden to the police, as they were professionals.

Mark was distraught, and after slipping into a panic attack, with his heart beating wildly and his breath coming in gasps, it was decided to call a doctor to attend to the young man, which Dorothy did.

Upon arriving at Dorothy's cottage, the physician injected Mark with a tranquilliser which took effect quite quickly, sedating him. His group of friends then helped him to a bed in Dorothy's spare bedroom where he soon fell asleep. Everyone was relieved, as it was distressing to see Mark so out of control – not that anyone else felt much better. They sat in Dorothy's lounge praying about the situation and talking – seemingly ever waiting for the telephone to ring, or for the police to once more knock at the door with, it was hoped, positive news concerning Eden.

Unfortunately, no such news was forthcoming. In fact, after four long days, the police had still not reported back, having been unable to track Eden, or her vehicle, down.

During this time, Mark had been admitted to the local medical centre which doubled as a small hospital of sorts, where he was now being kept under heavy sedation. A nurse was present at his bedside twenty four hours a day, to ensure the young man's safety during this horrific time.

Three nurses, each taking different shifts, sat with Mark continuously as he slept under the sedation given him.

In fact, two long weeks were to pass, before there was any news from the authorities concerning Eden.

During this time, the entire township came to know about her disappearance. There was an atmosphere of stunned shock among the residents as they wondered what had happened to the young lady whom many of them cared for.

After two weeks had passed, during which time Mark remained under sedation at the medical centre, two policemen visited with a group of Eden's friends with some news. Unfortunately, though, it was not the news that people had been hoping for – in fact, the report from the police was unexpected, as well as being extremely unsettling for Eden's friends to hear.

The policemen reported that Eden had finally been located in a large city some distance from the venue of the reunion, and, yes, she was alive. All of those gathered, breathed long drawn-out sighs of relief. However, no-one was prepared for what the police officer was to say next.

Eden was living in a small dwelling in this city, the constable stated. He then told them that, unfortunately, he was not at liberty to disclose the name of the city she was residing in. Also, he was not permitted to give out any information about Eden at all, except to say that she was alive and well. All that they could confirm, was that Eden had been spoken with by two of their colleagues and had requested that her whereabouts be kept undisclosed from those in her home town.

The silence that followed this statement was elongated as Eden's friends endeavoured to digest this information. Then followed a barrage of questions which were flung in disbelief at the policemen.

What had happened to cause Eden to not want to return home, as well as to refuse to allow those she loved to be informed of her whereabouts? Didn't the police know that she was engaged to be married? That this was out of character for Eden? The police were kind, although firm, replying that Eden was well and was living independently. They apologized for the fact that they were unable to disclose much information. They realized that every person in the room was stunned as well as completely baffled by what they had just been told. The policemen explained that, unfortunately, they had been given no choice but to respect the young lady's wishes to remain living in anonymity.

Many of those at the Centre began to become distressed. Mike Brewer asked that the policemen repeat all that they had said to them. He also could not believe that Eden would not want to return home to her fiance by choice, and he wanted to clarify that this was exactly what had been stated by the officers.

After once more explaining that Eden had indeed chosen not to return home, and had, in fact, initiated contact with the police herself when she learned that they were looking for her, instructing them to keep her whereabouts undisclosed, the two policemen, feeling a little uncomfortable at the obvious mix of pain and shock that their message had evoked, left the premises having once more apologized to those gathered.

After their departure, many unanswered questions hung in the air amidst an extremely long silence, while everyone uselessly endeavoured to make sense of that which they'd been told.

How could this possibly be true? There must surely be something more to the situation as this was not at all like the Eden they all knew and loved. Then everyone spoke at once, expressing their concern at the unbelievable report given them. It seemed to Eden's friends that they were merely a part of some awful movie, and that Eden would walk back into the room at any moment.

However, she did not. Neither did she contact anyone.

Approximately a week after having been given the news, Mark was released from the medical centre, an absolutely shattered and broken shell of a man.

CHAPTER SIX

As the days, weeks, and finally, months passed, the people of Shackellby Downes began to realize that their hopes of seeing Eden again were remote. Mark Hansen had completely withdrawn from the company of all of his friends, also shunning every social occasion in the town. He had stopped attending church services at the Centre, as well as having walked away from his job.

Totally consumed with grief, he was now rarely seen outside of his house, having become dependent on welfare payments in order to survive. To begin with, his friends had endeavoured to support and to encourage him. However, the young man had turned from every friendly hand.

Eventually, feeling useless, one by one, those in his circle of friends had left Mark to the hermit – like existence he seemed determined to live.

Each of his friends was deeply saddened to see him this way. However, he had consistently refused to allow them to be a part of his life. Finally, though, after nine or so months of living with an unbearable loneliness, Mark began to make an effort to rebuild his shambles of a life and to reconnect with friends as best he could. He had finally become unable to live his life in complete isolation for any longer. Having taken indefinite leave from his job, he now applied to return and was warmly received back at his place of work. As well as that, he was welcomed once more into his circle of friends.

Mark began to attend church meetings again, and made an effort to join in some of the community events, although, deep within, he was still numb with grief. He slowly came to genuinely enjoy times spent with friends once more, as many reached out to embrace him as well as assist him to pick up the pieces of his life – sadly, a life without the hope of Eden sharing in it.

However, in the depths of his heart, Mark remained shattered at the loss of the love of his life.

He made a silent vow never to marry another lady. From time to time, overwhelmed with secret sorrow, he would cry out to his God, pleading for Eden's return, as he clung even now, in a corner of his heart, against the odds, to the hope that somehow Eden would come home and back into his life. That she would arrive back in town, with some perfectly reasonable explanation as to why she had left home – left him.

Logically though, he realized that this possibility was remote, as much as he didn't want to admit it even to himself.

Since the time of Eden's disappearance, Dorothy Moore had been spending much time in prayer, while quietly shattered, herself, to have apparently lost the girl she looked upon as a daughter.

She missed their relationship which had been a close one.

Slowly, although many residents missed Eden's cherry

smile and loving personality, life in the Downes began to return to a normal kind of existence. The entire township was, however, mystified as to what could have possibly happened to prevent Eden from wanting to return home. This seemed, in the minds of the residents, to have been, on the part of Eden, a decision that was definitely out of character for the young woman to have made.

Why would she have done something like this? The report given by police did not somehow ring true, and was incomprehensible to many. This decision did not depict the Eden that so many of them knew and loved.

The town's folk wondered how she could have made such a decision, knowing that she would be hurting the people who loved her so dearly, especially Mark, as well as Dorothy and Vicky, on whose faces the strain was continuing to show. However, it seemed that there were no answers – at least none that seemed in the least bit plausible.

Although life in the Downes had regained a measure of normality, a question mark remained in the minds of all who felt that things were not quite as they seemed, although no-one had evidence to dispute the report of the police.

Meanwhile, the members of the town's local council were holding their monthly meeting on a Tuesday morning. Headed by Bob Fulton, they were heavily involved in a discussion as to how to increase the flow of visitors, as well as new residents, to the area. Ideas were being tossed around by council members, one of which had those at the meeting interested.

Morrie Whetton had presented the suggestion that a large indoor stadium be erected on a huge piece of council-owned land which was currently vacant. This stadium, Morrie explained, would seat up to four thousand people, and would be a perfect draw card for holiday makers. It would be an ideal venue for hosting large sporting events, as well as concerts and the like. Morrie went on to say that the building of this stadium could well assist in placing the small town on the map to a larger extent.

All of those present at the meeting agreed that this suggestion merited further discussion.

The meeting ended on a positive note, with plans to further discuss the idea at their next meeting.

Although Mark had returned to work, he was decidedly lacking in enthusiasm for the job that he had once enjoyed. He continued to silently grieve for the girl he still loved so very deeply.

Although life went on after a fashion for the young man, he felt that he would never be the person he had been before having lost Eden – that he had indeed lost everything.

He made an effort to remain an active member of the community as much as he was able to be. But his heart was broken and his thoughts consumed with an ongoing grief which continued to overwhelm him, despite his efforts to conceal it from those around him. He constantly worked at covering his sorrow, at least while in the company of others, but remained a deeply despairing man.

Meanwhile, Mike and Christine Brewer had decided to expand the Centre. They had instigated a plan to add another room to the building, and were calling upon locals to donate both their time and skills to assist with this project. As always, the residents quickly rallied around, with one local business promising to donate the entire amount of timber needed for the project.

It was hoped that the bulk of the labourers would be locals willing to give of their time, as well as the various skills, that many of them possessed.

Everyone gave willingly what they were able, with enthusiasm, and shortly work on the extension had begun, progressing quickly once started. Townsfolk worked tirelessly to enlarge the building that was used and loved by so many of them.

CHAPTER SEVEN

It was coming up five years since Eden's mysterious disappearance, and Mark Hansen was in a particularly low mood as he once again succumbed to a vicious form of depression. He sat slumped in an easy chair in his villa, leaning forward with his head in his hands, as he so often did these days. Although the years had passed, time had done little to dull the ache in his heart, as he continued to grieve for the woman he still very much loved.

Even after so long, there were many unanswered questions swirling in his mind, relentlessly tormenting him. Where was she? And why did she leave? Why had she not contacted him? These thoughts endlessly tortured him, even though he had, at least in part, resigned himself to the fact that he would now probably never know the answers.

In his ongoing sorrow, he had made a vow to never marry another woman. If he could not be with Eden, he would be alone.

In fact, Mark had recently once again taken to swallowing sleeping tablets, in an endeavour to obtain a measure of relief in sleep, during nights that often seemed endless.

The sleep that he did manage to get, was punctuated with nightmares about Eden. As he slept, he would many times see her in danger and reach for her desperately, only to lose his grip on her delicate wrist and watch her plunge over the edge of a cliff or fall into the path of an oncoming car. After such horrific dreams, having been jolted awake, Mark would often remain sleepless until morning, bathed in a cold sweat.

Many times, he was unable to quell the all too familiar panic that such nightmares would generate. Even worse, in many ways, were the pleasant dreams, during which he would dance with Eden, holding her close and kissing her gently. On these occasions he would awaken suddenly, usually in the early hours of the morning, shivering, as he realized that he was alone – that his mind had, once again, tricked him so cruelly. Mark was becoming increasingly angry – with the police, with God, and, yes, even, at times, with Eden herself, who, for some unfathomable reason, seemed to have wiped him from her life.

His misguided anger towards God caused him to withdraw from his Lord, even though he was dependent on God to take him through each day, leading him into a future that in many ways seemed to the young man to be almost devoid of hope. It wasn't that he did not do his best to continue to follow God as he endeavoured to ever push the anger he felt away. He even still attended the odd church gathering at the Centre. However, he had, as the years had passed, eventually become reclusive and uninterested in life to a large extent.

Even at his place of work, doing a job that he had once loved, he now found himself merely going through the motions, being often sleep-deprived, as well as feeling hollow inside.

Mark had once again become increasingly withdrawn, as the cruel depression he was suffering continued to hold him in a vice-like grip. He often remained isolated in the three-bedroomed villa he owned – the home that, alongside Eden, he had begun to renovate in readiness for Eden and himself to live in after their wedding.

These memories now, however, seemed to Mark to be another world away – one that had been cruelly snatched from him, robbing him of the contented peace he had once enjoyed in the company of the bright-eyed, energetic Eden. Now, he rarely laughed. In public he wore a plastic smile. Those who cared for him were once more becoming increasingly concerned for his health, both mental as well as physical, as his weight had plummeted.

He also appeared to be ever tired and drained looking. Most of the time, he would decline invitations from his friends to come for dinner, or to accompany them to see a movie.

His mind was almost always filled with thoughts of Eden, as he endeavoured to face a future in which he had chosen to live in solitude.

Even Mark's prayers had become a series of frustrated and tortured questions, as he cried on his knees, begging God to bring Eden home – asking Him to reveal to him where she was. Each night he would plead with God to give him the strength to make it through another day – another hour, and, at his worst, another minute.

In the midst of his distress, Mark barely noticed that all about him, the town had become a hive of activity and excitement, as the new stadium began to take shape. The council had decided to go ahead with the building of the stadium some months prior, and, with the foundations having been laid, work was now beginning in earnest on the huge project. Excitement among the residents was gaining momentum as they watched the building of this giant auditorium steadily progressing.

The labourers were kept amply supplied with delicious home baking as well as liquid refreshments, by locals, many of whom desired to play a part, no matter how small, in the bringing to birth of this ambitious project.

Meanwhile, many miles from the Downes, Eden McCabe stood silently facing a mirror. She was naked from the waist up, and she gripped a large carving knife which was poised at her chest. In an instant, she flung the knife to the floor, and slipping into a grubby skivvy, she buttoned a long black trench-like coat, up to her neck. She then walked briskly from the bedsit she was renting, to a nearby telephone booth.

Once there, Eden rummaged through her untidy handbag in search of a particular piece of paper. A photograph of Mark fell to the ground. Bending down, she quickly retrieved it, burying it once more in her bag. She then continued to rummage for the paper she was seeking.

Having finally found it, a crumpled page from a note book with a name and phone number scrawled upon it, Eden fed the phone's meter with coins.

Lifting the receiver from its cradle, she quickly dialed out, clutching tightly to the paper on which the number she was endeavouring to call was written.

CHAPTER EIGHT

Dorothy Moore quietly sighed. She had much on her mind. Today was the eighth anniversary of her beloved husband's death. She missed him still, so very dearly.

Usually positive in nature, Dorothy was struggling with discouragement today. She was weighed down – burdened with a sense of loneliness which she was finding difficult to shift. The walk home from town, which she had completed, armed with her supermarket shopping, seemed to have taken longer than usual. Indeed, today, Dorothy felt older than her sixty three years. Her late husband seemed to have been gone for more than eight years. On this particular day, Dorothy planned to visit the local cemetery later that afternoon. She was unusually sombre in mood. The steady rise of the driveway to her cottage seemed somehow steeper than usual, and she was grateful, upon reaching her front door, to drop her load of groceries, as she fumbled in her handbag for the keys to her house.

Dorothy's thoughts, once again, drifted to her husband. Their marriage, while certainly not perfect, had been filled with many special times, as this couple had truly been in love. Dorothy had weathered many storms with Graham at her side.

As a follower of God (which Graham had also been), Dorothy knew with certainty, that the couple would be reunited in heaven some day. However, this particular morning had been a long and tiring one. Upon opening the door to her home, Dorothy was greeted by the sound of the telephone ringing. A little breathless after her lengthy walk, she picked the receiver up and greeted the caller with a cheery hello. The person calling her was someone she had not been in contact with for some time, and, immediately, Dorothy, shrugging off her weariness, pulled up a chair for a brief, yet intense, conversation.

As she hung the receiver back up, she was relieved to have been at home and able to take this particular phone call during which she had scribbled some notes onto a note pad, which she kept beside the phone. She now pocketed the notes she had taken, then walked quickly into her bedroom. Opening her wardrobe, Dorothy pulled out an empty suit case into which she placed some items of clothing, as well as gathering a range of toiletries and a few other things. Glancing at her watch, she then made a telephone call to her close friend, Christine Brewer, with whom she spoke at length. Dorothy advised her friend that she would be travelling out of town for about a week. She confided in Christine the reason for her impromptu trip and requested that Christine and her husband, Mike, pray for her while she was away.

Dorothy then asked Christine if she would collect her mail, as well as keep a general eye on her property until she returned. Christine readily agreed, and the friends, having completed their conversation, said their goodbyes. After fixing herself a sandwich and a cup of tea, Dorothy loaded her bag, along with some blankets, into her small Suzuki Alto car. Then, having locked her home, she set off on her journey, heading out of town, via the north-bound motorway.

Dorothy's journey took her to a large city, many miles from her home town. The trip took her almost four days to complete. She drove each day until nightfall, booking into a motel to sleep, before setting off early each morning to continue her trip.

Finally, she reached her destination. After stopping to ask for directions several times, she arrived at the address she was seeking. After parking her vehicle on the road outside a dilapidated looking weatherboard dwelling, the small lawn of which was overgrown and unkempt, Dorothy walked through a gate which was barely hanging by a loose hinge.

She noticed that a flower garden at the front of the property had been badly neglected. Feeling a little uneasy, Dorothy knocked on the occupant's front door which was almost instantly opened. She gasped as she stared into the sunken and weary-looking eyes of Eden McCabe.

Although Dorothy had been aware that Eden would not be looking her best, she was appalled to see the extent of the younger woman's unkempt appearance and emaciated figure. It was apparent that Eden had not been caring for herself, as her hair hung in knotted clumps around her face.

As well as that, the unpleasant smell of body odour clearly indicated that Eden had not been attending to her personal hygiene for some time. Dorothy choked a little, biting hard on her lip, as she endeavoured to conceal her distress at seeing the girl she loved as a daughter in such a state of disarray. Tears filled her eyes, as her heart silently shattered. This was almost beyond what Dorothy could bare.

Eden ushered her inside, and the two women sat awkwardly in silence, facing one another on the only two seats in the small dwelling. Dorothy gently attempted to engage Eden in conversation.

In return, Eden spoke in a monotone, as well as with obvious reluctance. Her once dancing, fun-filled, hazel eyes, were almost void of expression. Dorothy wept a little as Eden's story came out, a little at a time.

Finally, at almost 10 pm, Dorothy stood to her feet, and reaching for Eden's arm, suggested that they book into a motel for the night before beginning the long journey home the following morning. In response, Eden nodded, and picking up her handbag, followed Dorothy to her vehicle without a word. Dorothy locked the door of the bedsit behind them, leaving the key in the property's letterbox which was in front of the rickety gate. As the two women drove off, both were silent, each preoccupied with their individual thoughts.

After checking into a nearby motel, Dorothy endeavoured to persuade Eden to have a shower, however, was unsuccessful in her bid. She wisely did not pressure the younger woman, and shortly after arriving at the motel, both retired to their bedrooms, with little hope of a quality sleep. In the privacy of her room, Dorothy got onto her knees, quietly praying as she silently wept before God. In fact, she continued in prayer for much of the night, while Eden, in the adjoining bedroom, tossed and turned, also finding sleep elusive.

Both arose the next morning, looking bleary-eyed and exhausted.

After a quick breakfast, Dorothy and Eden set off again, heading towards home. Sensing Eden's need for quietness, Dorothy kept conversation to a minimum, driving mostly in silence.

When they stopped for lunch, Eden merely picked at her food, eating very little as she pushed the food on her plate around with her fork. That evening, as the two women neared the place where they were to bed down for the night on the second day of their journey, Dorothy suggested that Eden move into 'Johnathon's bach', as she'd become used to calling it, where the younger woman would have some privacy.

This small, yet comfortable self-contained bach on Dorothy's section at the back of her cottage, had been built a number of years ago for the purpose of housing Dorothy's nephew, Johnathon, who had suffered from a severe form of depression.

After he had undergone years of treatment, Dorothy and her husband had persuaded the hospital authorities to allow her nephew to move into this purpose-built unit in which they'd hoped to provide Johnathon with some supervised independence.

Unfortunately, within just two years of having moved into his new home, he had tragically ended his own life. Since that time, the bach had remained unoccupied.

It was this flat which Dorothy intended to provide for Eden to reside in.

Finally, after travelling for almost four days, the two women arrived back at Dorothy's home.

Throughout the entire trip, Eden had been very withdrawn, which was of concern to Dorothy. She pulled into her driveway at approximately 10 pm, and parked her car in a garage to the side of her cottage.

Dorothy then, walking to the back of her property, unlocked the bach, and stood back to allow Eden to walk inside. She then handed Eden the key to her new home.

Dorothy had quickly prepared the bach for Eden's home-coming before leaving town. Good nights were exchanged, and, as Dorothy left Eden alone, the younger woman locked the door, then immediately pulled all of the drapes.

Eden's mind was in turmoil. "What now?" she wondered. Had she done the right thing in calling Dorothy to collect her? How could any part of her life ever possibly be restored? Eden was aware that she had become a completely different person. She no longer even prayed to the God she had once followed and loved with abandon.

Alone in her new home, she lay on top of the bed curled up in a fetal position.

With her thoughts running rampant, Eden was unable to sleep.

Meanwhile, back in the cottage, Dorothy was also somewhat relieved to be alone. She had much to think about. Her heart was troubled as she wondered how to even begin to assist in this young woman's healing journey. However, motivated by a fierce love for Eden, Dorothy was fully committed to walking alongside her younger friend on her road to recovery, knowing, also, that it would be a lengthy one, with no guarantee of success.

Dorothy realized, also, that professional help would be essential for Eden. She was aware, as well, that she was completely out of her depth in this situation. Dropping to her knees, she quietly prayed, handing the entire situation into the hands of her Heavenly Father.

CHAPTER NINE

Having allowed Eden a few days to settle in to her new home, Dorothy knew that the time had come to speak honestly with her, as well as maybe challenge her a little. Eden still had not showered or washed her hair. Neither had she done much more than pick at the meals that Dorothy had prepared for her. In fact, Eden hadn't left the bach since her return, neither had she opened the drapes of the little unit.

After a time of prayer, during which Dorothy asked for wisdom regarding the talk she was about to have with her young friend, she knocked on the door of what had become Eden's little hide-away. Eden opened the door with a barely audible greeting, and stepped aside to allow Dorothy to enter. "Sit down, Eden," Dorothy said. "I think it's time we had a talk." Without a word, Eden complied, and the two women sat in easy chairs facing one another. Dorothy spoke first, asking Eden what it was that the younger woman really wanted for her life – for her future – now that she was home once more. "I want to die," Eden mumbled her reply.

Dorothy responded with more than a little impatience. "Then why did you phone me and ask me to bring you home just for you to kill yourself?" She continued, "My goodness, Eden, weren't you already doing that while you were away?"

Lowering her eyes, Eden shrugged before replying, "I guess so," as tears began to form in her eyes and trickle down her face.

The walls that Eden had so carefully built around her heart were beginning to crack. This was the first sign of any form of emotion that Eden had shown since her return. Dorothy breathed a silent prayer of thanks to her God, before placing an arm around the now trembling Eden and drawing her close. "It's going to be all right, sweetheart," she soothed. "It might take some time but things will improve for you," she reassured the young woman.

Finally, Dorothy herself was beginning to believe the words that she had just spoken. That the breakthrough she'd been seeking for Eden, had begun with the tears that Eden was now shedding freely.

The ice was finally melting, and Eden was beginning to 'feel' once more. Dorothy held Eden to her chest as they both wept, Eden with pain, while Dorothy sobbed with relief. "No, my dear," Dorothy spoke again. "You didn't come home to end your life. You came because, deep within, you longed for love and healing from the people who care for you here. This is where you need to be," she stated. "Home with us."

Eden nodded slightly, then asked to be left alone for a while. "I'll leave you for a bit," Dorothy replied, "but not until you agree to allow me to wash your hair later this evening. You need to start letting us assist you to help yourself a little. Now, do we have a deal?"

Eden, looking anxious, shrugged, drawing back slightly.

"I know you have lived this way for some years now," Dorothy continued, "but you don't have to do this alone. I am here to help you. One step at a time is all I ask. You can take a shower tomorrow, but, Eden, I cannot allow you to continue neglecting yourself like this, no matter how dreadful you feel, or how much you have suffered. I love you as a daughter. I am going to bring some towels and shampoo across from the house later. I'm sorry but some of those knots in your hair will need to be cut out. Don't worry, I'm not too bad with the scissors. I used to cut Graham's hair," she explained. "I'll return at 8 pm and we will tackle that hair. Is that all right?" Dorothy asked.

Eden responded with a barely visible nod of the head.

As Dorothy prepared the evening meal, she felt a little unsettled, knowing that there were many other things that needed addressing with Eden.

One of these was Mark Hanson. He was aware, by now, that Eden had returned to the town, and was terribly distressed at not having been able to see her right away. Dorothy had persuaded him to wait a few days for a visit to be arranged. She had spoken a little with Mark, explaining to him that Eden had returned home a very troubled and disturbed young woman, and that there was need for careful planning concerning the timing of his visit.

Mark had reluctantly accepted that he would need to wait a few more days in order to see the woman he loved. He was concerned to hear that Eden had become so damaged, although he knew none of the details of this. However, he was ecstatic to discover that she was back home once more and that he would soon get to see her. He hoped to finally receive answers to the multitude of questions which had plagued him for almost five years. He phoned Dorothy often, as it became increasingly difficult for him to remain patient when he wanted so very badly to wrap his arms around Eden, whatever her condition.

Dorothy did her best to prepare him for the possibility that Eden would reject him. However, Mark was not willing to even entertain thoughts of that nature. He also refused to accept the possibility that Eden would refuse to see him. Dorothy, emotionally weary herself, decided to leave that particular conversation with Eden until the following day.

By 10 pm, as a result of Dorothy's handiwork, Eden's hair had been cropped, and following the application of two generous doses of shampoo and a conditioning treatment, her dark hair looked, as well as smelled, considerably nicer.

This was new territory for Eden. She felt a little awkward as she had been living with unclean hair for some years now. However, she admitted that her now silky locks felt nice after having been attended to.

Before retiring for the night, the two women agreed to a time the following morning at which Eden would take a shower. This was a little more challenging for the younger woman. It was also something that she wished to do unassisted, quickly turning down an offer of help from Dorothy who understood Eden's need for privacy. Dorothy agreed to remain in the small lounge room of the bach while Eden showered.

Consequently, the following morning, after an uneventful

night, she brought over the toiletries needed for Eden. After handing her a newly purchased set of outer clothes, as well as fresh underwear for her to change into, Dorothy discarded the filthy skivvy and undergarments that Eden had been attired in for so long, while the young woman showered.

After a short time, Eden emerged from the bathroom, a little anxious after having achieved the task of cleaning herself. Dressed in her new clothing – although she was adamant in her refusal to remove her long, black overcoat – she looked, as well as smelled, considerably cleaner, which pleased Dorothy. After all, it was a positive step, however small, and it was certainly progress, which Dorothy was well aware would be slow. The stench of body odour had been largely replaced by the aroma of the English Rose scented soap that Eden had used to shower herself.

The following day, it was time for Dorothy to broach with Eden, the sensitive subject of Mark Hanson, which she did with some trepidation. After entering the bach, Dorothy indicated to Eden to sit down, and after having done likewise, began to gently talk with the younger woman.

"It's time for you to begin to allow the people in this town who care for you, into your life once more," she said to Eden who, in reaction, began to tremble visibly. Dorothy continued to speak, saying that Eden needed to begin this new step by being willing to talk with Mark.

"No, not Mark!" Eden cried out, immediately wrapping her arms around her chest as if in defence. "Not Mark," she repeated. "I can't do it."

"Eden, love," Dorothy replied. "Listen to me." Dorothy

continued as Eden's eyes, filled with fear, briefly met hers. "You have no idea of how much Mark has suffered. He is beside himself, having grieved for you from the time you left, to this very day. You owe it to him to at least talk to him. It's time for you to become a little less selfish and wrapped up in yourself, as there are others who are hurting and Mark is one of them. He is distraught and hasn't got over losing you. You have no idea of just what an impact your disappearance has made upon that young man."

Dorothy continued to speak as Eden appeared to be gasping slightly for breath. "Eden, I know for a fact that Mark still loves you very much, and that his love for you has not changed at all. Your response to that is entirely your decision, but I must insist on your meeting with him and at least telling him about what has happened in your life during the years that you were missing."

Eden sat silently, staring at the floor as Dorothy continued to speak to her.

"In fact," Dorothy said, "I am making it a condition of your continuing to live here that you speak to Mark, as at the very least, he deserves some kind of explanation. Try to think about others, Eden, the ones that you have hurt beyond measure when you just disappeared without a trace. Also," Dorothy continued, "what about Vicky and the others at the Centre? You need to begin to slowly integrate back into society, and the best place that I know of for you to do that, is right here in Shakellby Downes where people love you."

Eden, looking frightened, shook her head vigorously.

Dorothy, in response, touched her arm, speaking gently as

one would to a small, terrified child. "I am not expecting you to do this quickly," she said, "as you didn't get into this state overnight. Your healing will take time, but I do insist that you speak with Mark – in fact, I have been in contact with him and have invited him over to visit with us tomorrow evening at 7.30."

Eden jerked her arm away in a panic, replying with the words, "I can't."

"Well, then, "Dorothy responded, "if you are not willing to even attempt to help yourself with our support, you might just as well return to your bedsit in the city, and continue to slowly kill yourself, as you were doing."

Eden shuddered at the thought and buried her head in her hands.

Dorothy spoke once more, "I'll leave you now to make your choice. It may seem hard, Eden, but, truly, I am loving you and helping to save your very life, the only way that I know how, but I cannot do it unless you begin to take some responsibility and to work with me. I will leave you now for a bit and will return once you have had some time to think about what I have said to you. Is that all right?" Dorothy asked.

Eden barely nodded her assent and Dorothy then left the bach, trembling a little herself.

Back in her cottage, Dorothy drew a long breath. Although it had been difficult for her to be so harsh, she knew, also, that she needed to be firm with the fearful young girl whom Eden had become if bringing her home was, in fact, going to be successful. She was also keenly aware of Eden's need for professional help. Indeed, Dorothy herself, at this time, needed the support of her friends, and soon after returning to her cottage, she phoned Christine Brewer to arrange a visit with her for the following morning. Eden had spoken briefly to Dorothy of some scarring which was apparently on the young woman's chest and shoulder area. She had stated that this was the result of some kind of incident in a kitchen en route to the school reunion, but had not gone into any detail regarding this. This scarring, in fact, was the reason Eden had given for her refusal to return home. She blamed it for her disappearance, as well as for the absence of all contact with those in her home town.

Dorothy had not sighted these scars. However, she gathered from the little that Eden had told her, that they were unsightly. Consequently, in her wisdom, Dorothy had refrained from pressuring Eden to show them to her, as it was obvious that the distraught state that Eden was now in, stemmed from the way the young woman felt about these scars on her body.

Dorothy felt suddenly quite weary. She realized that the journey back to health for Eden would be a lengthy one, with no guarantee of success. Still, in her fierce love for Eden, Dorothy determined that she would do everything in her power to assist her protégé to reclaim her health.

She would stand with Eden, supporting her as fully as possible in her healing journey.

Later that evening, after having visited with Eden once more, Dorothy, after having been given, although reluctantly, consent from the young lady, phoned Mark Hansen in order to confirm his visit for the following evening. She then, walking into her bedroom, dropped to her knees as she cried out to her God for the miracle that she knew would be needed.

CHAPTER TEN

The day of Mark's visit dawned, and he arrived at Dorothy's cottage promptly at 7.30 pm as arranged.

Unsure of what to expect, Mark was finding it difficult to contain the mix of emotions which threatened to overwhelm him as he knocked on Dorothy's front door with some trepidation.

Dorothy invited him in, and the two spoke privately for a short time before going to the bach to meet with Eden.

Both Mark and Eden felt awkward and somewhat ill at ease. However, Mark knew for certain that this was the woman that he was still very much in love with. Also, that he would stand with her whatever the implications of that might be.

Eden mumbled in reply to his quiet and gentle greeting, and the three people seated themselves.

The silence that followed was a little disconcerting for all. Mark furiously blinked back the tears that threatened to overwhelm him. Without warning, Eden stood to her feet, staring momentarily at Mark before turning her back on her visitors. She quickly removed her long trench coat as well as her tee shirt and undergarments. Then, naked from the waist up, she spun around to face Dorothy and Mark wearing an expression of defiance.

Dorothy and Mark gasped audibly as they sighted Eden's chest and shoulder areas. The skin covering much of her upper body was splashed with scar tissue, which, overtime, had become creamy-coloured, slightly raised areas upon her body. Across the front of her right shoulder, the skin was withered and uneven where a skin graft had not knitted successfully, leaving a slight hollow on the lower part of her shoulder.

However, it was not this scarring that arrested the attention of both Mark and Dorothy. Each of them was speechless at the sight of numerous slash marks and cuts overlaying the entire area of Eden's upper body. Some of the wounds stretched almost the full width of her chest.

Although many of these obviously self inflicted wounds had healed, or at least partially so, there were a number which had been recently inflicted, as they were still weeping and raw. It appeared that Eden had indiscriminately cut and hacked at her own body.

An elongated silence followed, before Mark spoke to Eden.

"You did this to yourself?" he asked incredulously, visibly shaken.

Eden nodded, avoiding his gaze. She then spontaneously folded her arms across her chest, as if to conceal her body, before addressing Mark. "See," she spoke angrily, almost accusingly. "Tell me just how much you love me now."

Mark walked slowly over to her consumed with the emotion he was unable to control.

Eden continued to speak, "I hated myself and I still do. The burn marks made me so ugly, no man would ever want me again, not you or anyone else."

Completely overwhelmed, she began to weep.

Eden addressed Mark again. "I knew that you would never see me as being attractive again and I couldn't bear to have you pity me."

Then, turning her back, she quickly clothed herself again before sitting silently, her eyes on the carpet. Mark slowly walked over to where she was seated and gently wrapped his arms around her trembling body.

"Look at me, Eden," he said.

Very slowly, she lifted her eyes to meet his. His eyes reflected tenderness and unfeigned love mixed with concern, as tears flowed down his cheeks unabated.

Eden stiffened a little at his touch.

He then leant over and whispered to her. "My precious Eden, you have been through so much, all alone, without support. How could you possibly think for a moment, that any amount of scarring on your body would make any difference at all to my love for you? You are, indeed, still the most beautiful girl that I have ever met, and also the woman I am very much in love with and attracted to."

Eden sat silently, stunned by this unexpected reaction from Mark. However, as she looked into his eyes, she knew that the words that he had spoken were genuine. She relaxed slightly as he held her.

"Tell me about it," Mark prompted gently.

After a moment, Eden hesitantly began to speak. She

explained that while en route to the school reunion over four years earlier, she had been burned as the result of a kitchen accident at a hostel she had booked into for the night. Hospital treatment had been required, including a small skin graft across the front of her left shoulder. This skin graft operation, unfortunately, had been unsuccessful. Overcome with horror upon viewing the unsightly burns, Eden had refused a second operation to repair the 'mess' left by the first graft.

She had then, against medical advice, discharged herself from the hospital. For a week or so after her exit from hospital, Eden had resided in a shelter for the homeless, suffering almost unbearably with the pain of the burns, even though she had been given a prescription by a doctor for medication to help with this pain. Having withdrawn much of the money saved in her bank account, Eden did not apply for welfare or other assistance.

She continued speaking. "I felt that the pain from the burns was a form of justified punishment – that I deserved it because I looked so ugly," she told Mark, while staring at the floor.

At this point, Dorothy quietly left the bach to give Eden and Mark some privacy, while Eden continued her story.

She had possessed only the items in her suitcase, as well as a long, black trench coat, which buttoned up to the neck. She had purchased this coat while living at the shelter, as it completely concealed her burns. Having moved into the tiny bedsit, which she had lived in for almost five years, Eden had gradually become bitter, as well as obsessed with her scarring, as the burns slowly began to heal. Self hatred had crept in, eventually swallowing her up.

Finally, she had begun to mutilate the newly healing areas on her body which had been burned.

Also, at that point, turning from society in general, she preferred to hide away as much as possible.

Sadly, she had also turned from the God whom she had once followed and loved with abandon, and had taken her anger at what she referred to as her disfigurement, out upon herself. "It was a type of deserved punishment. I felt somehow cleansed emotionally when I mutilated myself."

She continued speaking to Mark. "As if every time I cut at myself, I seemed to experience a kind of emotional release."

Over time, the compulsion to self-mutilate had intensified, until she was engaging in this destructive behaviour on a daily basis. Then, having become increasingly withdrawn, Eden began to live as a hermit, only leaving her bedsit when absolutely necessary. She also began to neglect her personal hygiene. Furthermore, in an attempt to punish herself more fully, she began to execute judgement upon herself in other ways, severely restricting the amount of food she permitted herself to consume. She had convinced herself that she, in fact, did not deserve to eat.

Indeed, both Dorothy as well as Mark, had been shocked to see how dreadfully thin she had become. Eden had gradually sunken into a dark and lonely depression.

"What brought you to the stage where you phoned Dorothy, asking that she come and collect you?

What was it that made you come home after all that time?" Mark enquired.

Eden was silent for a moment, unsure of how to express

herself, before answering. "I'm not sure," she replied. "I suppose that, although I had worked so diligently at hardening my heart and killing off all of my feelings and emotions, I wasn't able to do it fully. I couldn't quite quell the desire to be loved."

As well as that, Eden explained that quite regularly, while asleep, she would have dreams during which she would see Dorothy reaching for her. " At times," she said, "these dreams were so vivid that I would actually feel her arms around me, holding and comforting me – loving me – after which I would awaken suddenly, only to realize that I had been cruelly tricked, and was, in fact, still alone." Eden continued speaking. "The loneliness was awful," she explained. "I guess if I had been successful in deadening my feelings, I would quite probably have taken my own life.

However, somewhere in a corner of my heart, a little slice of hope must have remained despite my efforts to obliterate it. I truly believe that's probably the sole reason that I am still alive today."

Finally, Eden sighed. "There came a day when I just could not cope with the isolation and the loneliness anymore. It was at that time that I made the phone call to Dorothy, knowing that I could not carry on for much longer just merely existing."

Eden was silent and Mark responded. "Sweetheart," he said, "while you were missing, it was as though my very heart had been ripped apart. I've suffered so dreadfully as well, not knowing where you were or why you had seemingly abandoned me so very cruelly. Why did you not contact me, or at least ask someone at the hospital to do so when this accident first happened?" he asked her.

Eden hesitated, then responded. "I was in dreadful pain and the morphine injections that they were giving me caused me to hallucinate and confused my brain to the point where I couldn't think properly and was in and out of sleep constantly. I haven't much memory of my first few days in hospital even now. By the time that the dose had been sufficiently lowered, I had seen the awful disfiguring graft and had recoiled at the ugliness of it. I knew that I was now so badly disfigured that people would find me too unsightly to be around, especially you, Mark. The very last thing that I wanted was for you to feel obliged to stay with me out of pity, so I made the choice to cut all ties with everyone in the Downes."

Mark nodded his head in response, to indicate that he understood, but his voice trembled as he continued to speak out of his own pain. "I truly didn't believe that I would ever see you again."

His eyes filled once more with tears. In between sobs, he choked out his words. "I didn't know if you were even still alive, or why you seemed to have rejected me without reason."

He continued. "I've been living with a broken heart for all of these years. My life has been on hold, Eden." Mark paused then spoke again, "I despaired of ever seeing you again."

Finally, he asked a question of Eden. "Do you believe that I love you still – that I am so very much in love with you, despite all that has happened?"

Eden finally made eye contact with Mark, her own

emotions engulfing her. Looking into his eyes, she hesitated, then slowly nodded her head in response. She, indeed, realized that Mark was telling her the truth – that his love for her was genuine, even after all that they had both been through.

Finally, she allowed him to draw her close, and he wrapped her in his arms as they silently sat together on the couch. Eventually, Eden rested her head on Mark's shoulder.

Mark spoke again, asking a question of Eden. "Will you allow me to help you – to permit me to walk by your side once more, during your healing journey and beyond? Eden, will you once more be mine forever?" he asked, then continued. "I really couldn't cope with losing you again."

Eden hesitated before replying. "I don't know," she said, "I need time. You understand, don't you?" she asked Mark.

"Of course," Mark responded. "Take all the time that you need. Just holding you in my arms once more is enough for me right now."

The couple clasped hands, both emotionally exhausted, yet having made much progress during their time together.

Finally, Mark rose to his feet to leave.

After gently kissing Eden on the forehead, he reiterated the words that he had spoken earlier, telling Eden, once more, that he loved her and wanted to stay by her side. He added that he would not put pressure on Eden, but would be there for her as much as she would allow him to be. Mark then left, telling Eden that he would call in to visit with her the following day. The couple embraced and Mark walked out to his car. He was somewhat overwhelmed by what had been an emotionally intense visit.

Before driving off in his car, Mark spent a short time with Dorothy who was pleased to hear the hope and positivity in Mark's voice as he briefly told her of his time alone with Eden, as well as his intention to visit her the following afternoon.

Upon reaching his villa, Mark slept without the aid of sleeping tablets – a long, refreshing sleep.

At last he was free of the nightmares which had tormented him for so long.

Dorothy, following a short time of prayer, prepared for bed. She, too, slept soundly and peacefully.

The next morning, Mark was enjoying a hearty breakfast when his telephone rang. He answered cheerfully, feeling relaxed, and rested. The caller was Dorothy Moore, and the words she spoke sent shivers throughout Mark's entire body.

A breathless Dorothy, obviously panic stricken, spoke rapidly to Mark. "It's Eden. She's gone. Her bed hasn't been slept in, and her suitcase and belongings are missing. Oh, Mark!" she cried in despair. "I think she's run off again."

CHAPTER ELEVEN

Mark Hansen was distressed, as well as deeply frustrated at the news that Eden had once more gone missing. He punched at the air with his fist. However, uppermost in his mind was the thought that he must find her, and that, as quickly as possible. But where was he to even begin searching? Dorothy, who had phoned Mike and Christine Brewer immediately after having called Mark, now phoned again with a plan of sorts.

She told Mark that she would drive around the central areas of the township, while Mike and Christine were to cover the roads around the bush areas. To Mark, Dorothy assigned the streets on the outskirts of town, including the railway and bus terminals, as well as the roads out of town.

Grateful for some direction, Mark, after quickly dressing, jumped into his car and headed north. He prayed as he drove, as did the others, asking God to direct them to wherever Eden was.

Mark drove a little aimlessly, feeling deflated, as though on a hopeless mission. By now she could be anywhere. He knew for certain, that whatever happened, he would not give up on his quest to find Eden. He would not be able to cope with losing her again. This made him determined to track her down. In the far recesses of his mind lay the disturbing thought that Eden may have taken her own life. As a result, he prayed more intensely as he pleaded with God to keep her safe until she could be found.

Finally, having driven for almost an hour around the outskirts of town, Mark pulled over to the side of the road, desperately trying to clear his mind. He rested his head in his hands, as he endeavoured to gather his thoughts. He was almost out of ideas. "What now?" he silently asked himself.

Then he decided to search the local railway station which was, by now, little more than a dilapidated old building and virtually unused. He realized that he had little hope of finding Eden there. As expected, the train station was deserted.

Taking a deep breath, Mark turned his vehicle around and headed for the depot from which buses arriving in and departing from the small town, picked up and dropped off passengers. This service, too, had been radically cut back, with most people now preferring to travel by car, using the new motorway as access to and from the Downes.

Mark parked his car and scanned the front of the old wooden building which also seemed to be silent and empty. As he turned to walk around to the back of the building, he suddenly stopped, as his attention was arrested by a small noise. It seemed to be coming from the area of the toilet facilities at the side of the depot.

Standing still, he listened intently, and again heard the sound. It was a kind of a whimper, similar to that of a small, injured animal. Running over to the partially closed door to the toilet block, he flung it open.

Sitting on the floor, beneath a row of hand basins with her suit case beside her, was a sobbing and shaking Eden.

With a mix of relief as well as unexpected anger, Mark shouted at her. "What do you think you are doing?"

Then immediately calming himself, he reached for the weeping woman and helped her to her feet. He held her close as if afraid that she would disappear again from before his very eyes.

"Are you hurt?" he questioned her.

Eden replied with a timid, "No." She endeavoured to speak as her weeping intensified. "I – I'm so sorry, Mark. Please forgive me," she sobbed. "It was all too much for me last night – I felt overwhelmed and confused," Eden's words tumbled out. "I don't know how to cope any more with people – with being loved. I just had to get away as I truly didn't know what else to do."

Eden resembled a frightened child as she became increasingly distressed.

She continued to speak to Mark. "I ran away on impulse. I've despised myself for so long now. Please don't be angry with me," she pleaded.

Mark spoke gently to her. "I'll take you home now and prepare you some food."

He continued to talk in a soothing voice, aware that Eden was extremely vulnerable at this time. "You are safe with me and I will not abandon you. Will you come with me, Eden?" he asked.

Eden nodded in reply, an expression of relief spreading across her face as she clung to Mark.

Mark laid an arm across her shoulder. Then, picking up her suitcase with the other hand, they slowly walked together to his car. Eden was shivering, due, in part, to the chilly weather, but also to the mix of emotions which were churning inside her.

She tried again to express herself. "I don't know how to accept love from people any more, or how to give it. Also, I'm not able to cope with even being among people now. I really don't know what to do." She began to sob once more.

Mark replied, softly reassuring her. "We will help you to learn, but, Eden, I need you to make me a promise." Mark continued speaking. "Will you promise me that you will never run from us again? Can you do that?"

Eden hesitated, then whispered her reply. "You have my word."

They drove in silence, both preoccupied with their individual thoughts. Mark's mind swirled with unexpressed anxiety as he pondered on how complicated things were becoming with Eden. He wondered also, what lay ahead for Eden as well as those who loved her, including himself. He knew for certain that the immediate future would not be an easy one to navigate as he walked alongside Eden, who had not yet even begun her journey towards health. However, he remained fully committed to standing beside the woman he loved, regardless of the personal cost to himself.

Mark finally parked his vehicle in front of Dorothy's cottage. Dorothy's car was parked outside as was that of Christine and Mike Brewer.

Leaving Eden in the car, he quickly walked up to the front door and knocked loudly before walking in. Those gathered inside looked at him somewhat nervously. He rapidly filled them in on the events that had unfolded, telling them that Eden was safe and was now home once more.

All were tremendously relieved, and Mark once more went out to assist Eden into the house.

Carrying her suit case, he walked with her inside where she once again broke down.

Amidst a flood of tears, she spoke to those assembled in Dorothy's lounge, expressing her sorrow at having caused them such worry.

Following reassurances from those present, Dorothy wisely suggested that the young woman retire to the bach in order for her to obtain some much needed sleep. After Eden had rested, they would talk.

Eden complied with gratitude and Dorothy walked with her around the house to her little unit.

After slipping into some night wear, a subdued and exhausted Eden climbed into bed, quickly succumbing to sleep.

Dorothy left the bach to rejoin those at her cottage. They discussed the situation over coffee.

Everyone agreed that a structured plan for Eden's recovery was needed. However, Dorothy cautioned those present, stating that, because Eden had become so very damaged, she was particularly vulnerable at this time. They would all need to be sensitive and, at least for now, move at Eden's pace, which would be slow – probably painfully so at first.

Everyone agreed, and after a short time of prayer, Dorothy's guests dispersed, having made an agreement to meet again the following morning for prayer and further discussion.

They were all encouraged by the fact that Eden had been found and, also, that she had willingly returned home.

At the same time, each person realised that the weeks and months ahead would be difficult, requiring perseverance and patience on the part of each of them.

Eden slept soundly throughout the night, only waking when Dorothy arrived with her breakfast the following morning.

After Eden had showered, albeit reluctantly, Dorothy changed the dressings on her wounds. She applied antibiotic cream and sterile gauze which she taped over the areas which were still raw. Thankful for the nursing experience she had acquired earlier in life, she was pleased to see that the welts on Eden's body were improving now that they were being regularly attended to. The fact that Eden was finally keeping herself clean was also helpful, contributing, in part, to the success of her body's healing.

Dorothy carefully applied fresh dressings, keeping an eye out for any signs of infection. However, the wounds were healing nicely, although there would be horrific, angry, red scarring, which would, to a large extent, remain. This scarring would probably mar Eden's upper body for the rest of her life. Dorothy was aware that the more difficult scars to deal with would be the emotional and mental ones.

In fact, the time was shortly to come, when Eden would need to begin meeting for sessions with a professional counsellor. This counsellor would have to be chosen carefully, as it was important for Eden to meet with exactly the right person to work with her on the major problems in her life. She would need to be a compassionate, yet firm, person. Someone who would assist Eden to regain healthy emotions as well as the self worth she had been stripped of. Ideally, this counsellor would also be a Christian.

Dorothy knew that the months to follow would be extremely difficult and intense ones for Eden, having lived with much self hatred for some years now. She would require assistance to re-integrate little by little back into society.

Dorothy sighed, suddenly feeling weary. After all, there were no guarantees that Eden would be able to cope with all of the changes that needed to take place. No certainty that she wouldn't just quit and shut down emotionally again. Yes, Dorothy mused, every piece of ground gained would be hard fought for.

Dorothy hoped that Eden would be motivated to see the journey through with the encouragement and support of those who loved her. Consistent prayer was vital. If not for the greatness of God's love and power, there would be little chance of a successful outcome.

Dorothy breathed a silent prayer. "Thank you, Lord, that you are so big. We need you so much now."

Lost in her thoughts, she was startled by the sound of Eden speaking to her. She was asking Dorothy if Mark was going to call in that day for a visit. "I'm sure he will," Dorothy replied. "He's taken leave from work especially to spend extra time with you."

"I'm glad," Eden responded with a hesitant smile.

Dorothy glimpsed the hint of a sparkle in her eyes. At this time, any glimmer of improvement displayed by the young woman was pleasing to see, and Dorothy was encouraged.

CHAPTER TWELVE

Dorothy smiled as she scanned the shopping list that Eden had prepared for her. Nail polish, hand and body lotion. In large letters, underlined, were the words, 'rose scented.' The list continued.

Eyebrow tweezers, mascara and, in brackets, 'black'. There were several other items as well.

Dorothy was encouraged greatly to see that Eden had finally begun to pay a greater amount of attention to her personal appearance.

Tucking the young woman's list into a side pocket in her handbag, she promised Eden that she would obtain the purchases while in town that morning.

"Oh," Eden interjected. "I also need some hair ties – blue, if you can get them."

"Yes, my dear," Dorothy replied with a mock salute, and the two women erupted into laughter. Dorothy gazed for a few moments at her protégé, before asking her a question. "You wouldn't be making yourself glamorous in order to impress a certain young man named Mark now, would you?"

"I might be," Eden conceded, with a slightly embarrassed grin.

"Where is he taking you tonight?" Dorothy asked. "Somewhere special?"

"Maybe," came the noncommittal, slightly mischievous reply.

Dorothy's heart sang. It was good to see that Eden had become, by this time, considerably brighter and more contented, as well as seeming to have regained a greater degree of contentment in general.

The last twelve or so months, as expected, had certainly been difficult for Eden, as well as for those supporting her. However, the tide seemed to be finally turning as she exuded a new found sense of inner peace, as well as the much welcomed return of a mischievous sparkle in her piercing hazel eyes.

Eden had been meeting for sessions twice weekly with a therapist by the name of Rosemary Paddon, for twelve or so months now, and, at this time, was continuing her therapy with this lady. She had quickly formed a bond with Rosemary, and had come to trust and value her.

Progress, when it had begun, had been rapid, and Eden had just lately begun to display a newly emerging sense of confidence, especially in the area of her body image. This was something that had come to pass more quickly than expected, although, all too soon, her progress in this area was to be severely tested.

By this time, Eden had begun to experiment with her clothing choices, wearing pretty colours once more, as well as having discarded the dreadful, black trench coat in which she had attired herself constantly for some years. Eden had also begun to wear, on a regular basis, bright skirts and matching blouses, even though some of her scarring was exposed in these clothes.

These were certainly huge steps for Eden to have taken, and a battle still in the process of being bravely fought by the young woman, supported by those who loved her. All were pleased with her progress. She had, once again, been spending a large amount of time in the company of Mark Hansen.

It was obvious to many who knew the couple, that their relationship had once more become special to both of them. They were immensely enjoying the time that they spent together once more as a couple.

Meanwhile, Dorothy returned from her morning shopping expedition, only to discover Eden rummaging frantically through her wardrobe.

Six or seven items of clothing had been tossed haphazardly across the bed. She looked at Dorothy while explaining that she didn't know what to wear that evening on her date with Mark.

Dorothy replied smiling, "That's obvious, my dear." She then suggested several outfits to Eden that she considered to be suitable.

However, the young woman denounced all of Dorothy's suggestions for one reason or another.

Finally, Eden picked out a blue silken dress, which she had not noticed hanging near the back of her wardrobe.

"This will do," she smiled, holding it up for Dorothy to admire. "My black heels will go with this perfectly," she exclaimed.

Dorothy was pleased. "Crisis over then," she stated. "You have chosen well, my dear," she said. "You do look extra beautiful in blue as it brings out the colour in your eyes."

Dorothy spoke again. "By the way," she told Eden, "I've managed to purchase everything on your shopping list."

"Great!" Eden was enthusiastic as she took the packages from Dorothy. "Let's have a bite of lunch," Dorothy suggested and the two women sat down to eat some hastily prepared sandwiches over at the cottage.

"Where did you say that Mark was taking you tonight?" Dorothy asked of her protégé. To which Eden replied that she hadn't said. Dorothy remained silent and, after having eaten their lunch, the pair attended to the dishes.

Mark arrived that evening to collect Eden for their date at 7.30 sharp.

"You look stunning, sweetheart," he greeted her, and hand in hand, they walked to his car.

"Don't wait up." Eden flung the words over her shoulder at Dorothy as they left, a cheeky grin on her face.

Climbing into Mark's vehicle, and after a quick wave to Dorothy who was standing in the doorway of her home, the two drove off.

"Young people," Dorothy muttered as she smiled with a contented sigh, and reclining in an easy chair, picked up the novel she'd been wanting to finish reading for about a week now. A quiet night was just what she needed, and decided that a cake of chocolate and a good book would fit the bill nicely.

Around midnight, as Dorothy was preparing for bed, she

heard a frantic pounding on her front door. Surprised, she opened it to be greeted by an excited Eden who was barely able to contain herself. Eden's words tumbled from her lips as she spoke in a flurry of sentences to Dorothy.

"Oh, Dorothy," she spoke rapidly. "It's so exciting, it's so great to be alive. Guess what?" she said to the older lady who wasn't sure what was about to be virtually screamed at her in Eden's fever-pitched voice.

"What is it?" Dorothy asked, smiling to see her protégé looking so radiant about something.

Anything was possible with Eden these days. "You might have to just spill it out," she suggested laughing a little herself.

Eden, after wrapping her arms around the woman she loved as a mother, stood back a little before speaking again. Drawing a deep breath in an effort to contain herself, Eden spoke again, her hazel eyes sparkling. "I know it's late but I just had to tell you this amazing news. Oh, Dorothy," she blurted out, Mark has proposed to me again and I've accepted."

"Sweetheart, what can I say?" Dorothy answered, not especially surprised, having guessed that this time would come sooner rather than later.

"Congratulations, pet." She hugged Eden warmly. "I am so very pleased for you both."

Dorothy invited the younger woman in and the two sat in conversation until the early hours of the following morning – Eden, not surprisingly, doing much of the talking.

Finally, with Eden having retired to her bach for what was left of the night, Dorothy prepared for bed, extremely glad to see the enormous amount of progress that Eden had made and, also, excited herself at the thought of an upcoming marriage for Eden and Mark. She shook her head slightly as she climbed into bed having spent a few minutes in prayer before doing so. Both herself and Eden found it difficult to wind down for sleep that night.

CHAPTER THIRTEEN

News of Eden and Mark's engagement spread quickly amongst the townsfolk, and many were quick to offer their congratulations to the couple. Also, at this time, a new and widespread wave of excitement was sweeping through the people of Shackellby Downes. The much awaited grand opening of the recently completed new stadium was now less than a week away.

'Mount Stadium' as it had been named, was due to be officially opened in just six days time.

The town's mayor had managed to secure the services of a world-renowned prophet, by the name of Geoff Steadman, to speak at the venue's opening ceremony. Mr Steadman was currently holidaying in the area, and had readily agreed to be the guest speaker for the evening. This stadium was indeed an impressive sight, dwarfing the area surrounding its massive bulk. The huge structure contained seating for up to four thousand people. Tickets for the opening night were being swallowed up by locals and visitors alike. Many proud residents had invited friends and relatives from out of town to attend this landmark event. Everyone, it seemed, desired to be involved in the opening ceremony. Although far from it being filled to capacity, most of the town's folk would be in attendance, including the local media team.

The countdown to its grand opening was finally on, with excitement at an all time high. When Saturday evening arrived, people began flooding from early evening through the gates of the arena, eager to secure seats close to the front. Eden and Mark were also at the event, even though Eden generally still shied away from crowded places. A makeshift platform had been erected, on which Mr Steadman would stand to address his audience.

Soon after the people had finished crowding into the building, the evening began with the mayor cutting a white ribbon which stretched the entire width of the inside of the stadium. Immediately, a host of applause and cheering rang out from the crowd gathered. The evening's guest speaker was then enthusiastically welcomed.

Mr Steadman, formally dressed in a black suit, white shirt and plain blue tie, was a tall, thin man in his late fifties, with closely cropped greying hair. He waved in greeting to those gathered before requesting that they be seated. Mr Steadman then addressed the crowd. He spoke for almost forty-five minutes before inviting those who wished to be prayed for, to come forward.

Immediately, people began leaving their seats. It wasn't long before a lengthy queue had formed in front of the prophet.

Eden and Mark were among those requesting prayer. They desired that Geoff Steadman pray a blessing on their impending marriage. As it was warm inside the building, with humidity high, Eden slipped her cardigan off resulting in the exposure of much of her scarring. Although still a little nervous, by now she was beginning to get used to her scars being seen in public, although this confidence was still in its early stages. It was a major improvement for Eden, and no small feat for her to allow them to be exposed in the midst of such a large amount of people. Actually, she felt considerably less confident than her appearance suggested, but she was ever pushing herself in her recovery, to gain ground whenever she could. Her determination to recover was driven by a newly emerging anger within, at all that she had allowed herself to be robbed of for such a lengthy time. This anger motivated her to strive constantly in an endeavour to reach for full emotional health.

Those who knew Eden well, were aware of how difficult this was for her, and were extremely proud of her stubborn persistence, as well as of her attempts to overcome her problems at every opportunity. She consistently refused to cave in.

Microphone in hand, Mr Steadman began to pray, one by one, for those standing before him.

Finally, Eden and Mark's turn came. As they were about to ask him to pray over them, the prophet stood over Eden and asked her a question.

"Young lady," he asked. "What is your name?"

A blushing Eden stammered her reply.

Geoff Steadman continued speaking. "I believe that God has laid a message on my heart for you," he explained.

The entire auditorium became completely silent immediately, as everyone in attendance listened intently.

The members of the media pressed closer, holding their microphones as closely as possible to Mr Steadman, while their cameras snapped.

The prophet continued speaking to Eden. "God has given me a message for you," he stated. "You will be fully healed by the day of your wedding."

People in the audience, as well as both Mark and Eden, gasped audibly, as Eden had not even mentioned as yet to Mr Steadman that she and Mark were to be married. Mr Steadman then laid his hands upon the couple and prayed for God's blessing to be upon them.

The media had become ecstatic – this was definitely something out of the ordinary, and would make an excellent news story. They took photographs of Eden and Mark standing with the prophet, as well as some close-up ones of Eden, capturing her scarring on film as she desperately attempted to pull her cardigan back on.

After managing to escape from the gaze of the entire crowd, Eden, hating the spotlight, leaned up to whisper in Mark's ear, her eyes filling with tears. "Let's get out of here," she pleaded.

Mark, taking her arm, ushered her through the crowd and out of the stadium, concerned for his fiancée.

The couple quickly left in Mark's vehicle, driving to the reserve where Mark had proposed to Eden. Finally, they were alone and Eden broke down, wracked with sobs, while Mark did his best to comfort her. The couple spent about an hour together, hand in hand, walking a little as well as sitting on the wooden bench-like seats which were scattered around the area.

This park-like reserve had become a favourite for Mark and Eden as a place to spend time alone.

The evening had been an overwhelming one, especially for Eden, and the couple did not speak a lot to one another. Both were relieved to be alone together and away from the congestion of the crowded stadium.

Finally, with his arm around Eden's slim shoulders, Mark walked her to his car and they drove to Dorothy's home in silence. Eden was very subdued, which, although understandable given the circumstances, concerned Mark. He wondered if the events of the evening would disrupt her recovery. And if so, to what extent? Before leaving for the evening, Mark did his best to comfort and to reassure Eden, promising his support and reinforcing his love for her.

Just as Mark was leaving, Dorothy arrived home, also worried about Eden after her unexpected burst of publicity. She knew immediately that her protege was far from settled, and she held Eden's trembling body close. Eden then asked to be excused and, after reassuring Mark and Dorothy as much as was possible that she would be okay, retired to her bach for the night.

As expected, the front page of the town's local newspaper the following morning, was liberally splashed with pictures of Eden, her scarring prominent. There was also a photo of Geoff Steadman with his hands upon Mark and Eden.

If anyone had missed the stadium's opening ceremony, they were certainly filled in by this follow-up highlight. Beneath the pictures was a long article about the prophecy that had been given to Eden, under the attention-grabbing heading written in large letters: Prophet Predicts Miracle Healing.

The story of the previous evening's prophecy was embellished and written about in detail. It told almost all of Eden's story, beginning with how she had been missing from the town and had eventually turned up with the massive amount of scarring which was prominently displayed in the paper for all to see.

The newspaper also informed the locals of the date of Eden and Mark's wedding, which was now approximately three months away. The last paragraph of the article spoke a little about Mr Steadman, mentioning his widely acclaimed credentials as a prophet of God. The article ended with the question asking if this outrageous prophecy could possibly come to pass as Mr Steadman had predicted. Upon briefly sighting the pictures of herself in the paper, Eden, with a gasp, turned and retreated immediately to her bach, where she remained for the entire day, refusing to eat and allowing only Mark access.

Mark spent much time that day comforting as well as reassuring his fiancée that she was beautiful, regardless of her scars, while Eden fought to process the happenings of the previous night, as well as to digest the awful reality of the photographs and article presented that morning in the daily rag. "It will be okay, sweetheart," Mark promised a distressed Eden. "This publicity will quickly die down, you will see."

He soothed Eden while she clung to him. "We will get through this together," Mark promised. "You are not alone any more."

He attempted to joke a little in order to obtain a smile from Eden.

"Did you know that I am actually a ferocious lion in disguise and I will take care of you?" he asked her. She smiled a little in spite of herself.

Finally, the couple embraced, and Mark left the bach to allow Eden to rest. He was encouraged to see that, after his time with Eden, she seemed to be considerably brighter, however, was still opting for virtual solitude.

Those who were close to Eden were quite angry about the circumstances which had unfolded, especially about the newspaper article. They all did their best over the following days, as Eden slowly emerged from hiding, to reassure her that another piece of juicy gossip would quickly capture the attention of the townsfolk. However, most of the residents did not forget about this prophecy, although they began, over time, to stop discussing it as life in the town moved on. Many residents tucked it away in the back of their minds until the day of the wedding came, when they would be able to see for themselves whether the prophet's words would come to pass or not.

Meanwhile, as things settled down, Eden and Mark, with support from family and friends, continued with their wedding plans. Eden gradually recovered from the effects of her ordeal. However, her step lacked its usual bounce. As she became more cheerful, Dorothy was pleased, as she had also been quite concerned for the young woman to have had to endure this experience whilst still recovering.

Once things had settled a little for her, Eden, along with Mark, became quite enthusiastic once more as wedding plans again were brought to the forefront of their minds. It seemed as time passed, that Eden was navigating her way through well, what could have been a huge stumbling block for her. It appeared that the strength she had built up over the preceding year or so, was standing her in good stead. Those who loved and supported her were relieved, as this could have become a major setback for Eden. It seemed as the weeks finally began to pass, that all was well.

CHAPTER FOURTEEN

Walking arm in arm with her cousin, Vicky, through the mall, Eden was sporting a glistening solitaire diamond on her ring finger. Since the time that Mark had purchased it, Vicky had admired it many times.

"It's an absolute beauty," she commented, glancing at it yet again, "and just the right one for you," she said to Eden.

Eden just grinned, although she was finding it difficult to contain her excitement. She spoke to Vicky. "I didn't ever imagine that life for me would ever become as fulfilling as it is at the moment."

"I'm glad to see you so much happier," Vicky responded.

Eden smiled shyly, and the cousins sat talking for a while.

Vicky had agreed, with delight, when Eden had asked her to be the sole bridesmaid for the young woman's wedding. She had, however, stipulated that she would not be outfitted in any shade of pink.

Eden had jokingly suggested that she might have Vicky dressed in grey. Vicky snorted in reply, screwing her face up in mock horror.

Vicky, her mood changing, hesitated before speaking again to Eden.

"How are you now after all of the events at the stadium?" she asked her cousin, testing the waters a little.

Eden made a face. "I'm not sure," she replied. "I'm working with Rosemary, my therapist, on some issues that have arisen because of that evening."

Vicky nodded and paused before asking another question of Eden. "You are still sure, aren't you – I mean about the timing of the wedding?"

In reply, Eden nodded her head vigorously. "Of course," she said, "Whatever happens, I am going to marry Mark in just under two months now."

Vicky suddenly jabbed Eden in the ribs and whispered, "Veronica Hartly's heading this way and she is looking at you. Let's make ourselves scarce."

Eden quickly agreed and the two young women, stifling their laughter as best they could, hastily moved off, brushing passed an indignant Veronica, who had, indeed, been walking over to chat to them.

Shortly afterwards, the cousins parted company as Eden had some personal shopping to take care of, while Vicky was meeting a friend for lunch.

Eden visited several stores before heading home. Dorothy was involved in attending to some house work when Eden arrived at the cottage, so the young lady retreated to her bach where she laid some of the items she had purchased in town, onto her bed before placing them carefully on a shelf in her wardrobe. She smiled quietly, as she thought about Mark.

That particular day was Eden's afternoon for therapy. She drove to her appointment with Rosemary shortly after having eaten lunch.

Dorothy and Mark had travelled up to retrieve Eden's car a week or so after her return to the Downes.

They had been pleasantly surprised to have found it uninterferred with and in good condition.

However, Eden, who had been generally lacking in confidence at that time, had not driven it for at least three months after her return home.

Now she was grateful for the independence that her vehicle afforded her, and she was now meeting with her therapist unaccompanied. She was able to make her way to the sessions without having to rely on anyone to transport her to and from them.

The meeting that day left Eden feeling drained. Rosemary worked her hard, drawing out further emotional baggage from Eden's past, which still needed sorting in the young woman's life. The two worked intensively together, delving further into the many unresolved problems which had taken root during Eden's growing up years. It had been during those years, that Eden's low self-esteem, as well as a large amount of her insecurities, had been given birth to.

Meanwhile, the new stadium had secured its first booking from out of town. A band named 'The Crossroads,' a fairly popular one at that, was to perform in just six weeks time along with two smaller support bands. This upcoming event was drawing a large number of people from out of town and locals were also excited. Tickets for the concert were selling quickly, and it seemed that quite a crowd would be in attendance.

Eden's mind, however, was on other matters. Thoughts of her wedding day both plagued and excited her. She wondered with more than a little trepidation, if anything had been forgotten in the ongoing planning for the big event. In fact, she barely noticed the buzz of anticipation around her, as she continued preparing for her and Mark's ceremony. It was a little unnerving to realise that their wedding was now less than eight weeks away.

Being somewhat of a perfectionist, Eden was hoping, as well as praying, that all would come together perfectly. By this time, she had begun visiting her local hair salon on a regular basis, for conditioning treatments for her hair. Being already in good condition, her curly locks were becoming increasingly glossy as well as soft. She planned to have her hair trimmed about a week before the nuptials.

These were busy times for Eden and Mark, as well as for those assisting them with preparations.

Mark had invited his cousin, William, who lived some distance away, to be his best man at the ceremony. As the cousins hadn't been in contact for some time, Mark was pleased when William agreed to the proposal.

Never having met Eden, he grilled Mark about his wife to be, and the two men spent much time talking to one another by telephone, with Mark also catching up on some family news.

His parents were to be at the wedding, although they were not a close knit family. Mark's parents planned to visit two weeks prior to the ceremony in order to meet Eden. It had been decided that Mark and Eden would have a meal with them at a local restaurant.

Eden was apprehensive about meeting Mark's parents. However, Mark was quick to reassure her, saying that she would more than meet with their approval. Still, as the night approached, she fussed a little, trying to decide on an outfit that would be suitable to wear to the restaurant at which they were going to gather together for dinner.

Finally, Eden decided to go for a dressy-casual, light blue blouse, and a cream skirt, choosing cream coloured shoes with a small heel to complete the outfit. Despite Eden's concerns, the evening went extremely well. As Mark had predicted, his parents were drawn to the caring girl whom he had chosen to be his life's partner. It was clear that Eden adored their son and they heartily welcomed her into the family.

Mark's parents returned home the following day, looking forward to returning for the wedding. Eden had been given their seal of approval as a suitable bride for their youngest son.

These were stress-filled weeks for the couple as the venue for the wedding photographs was decided upon, along with seating arrangements for the various guests at the reception.

After the ceremony and the wedding reception, the wedding guests would move on to enjoy a relaxing evening at the Centre which was being 'made over,' with many assisting with this task for the big occasion.

As the weeks seem to pass quickly, almost before they knew it, only twenty six or so hours remained before Eden and Mark would marry.

Catering arrangements had been finalised as had all other items on the wedding check list.

Twenty four hours before the nuptials were to take place, Eden, with Vicky and Dorothy in tow, headed to a local motel which had been pre-booked in order to prepare in secret for the all important event. Of course, the whereabouts of this motel was a closely guarded secret.

Rising again in the minds of many of the locals, were thoughts regarding the prophecy given by Geoff Steadman to Eden, as the big day was now so close. Everyone, it seemed, was talking about the wedding, with more than a few wondering if this prophecy would, indeed, be fulfilled.

They were, at last, shortly to find out.

CHAPTER FIFTEEN

The day of Eden and Mark's wedding arrived with the sun rising early, bringing with it the much hoped-for provision of a fine day. An early morning chorus of birds donated nature's perfect choir, as if to usher in the ceremony which was set down for 2 pm that afternoon. It seemed that God, Himself, had personally gifted this couple with a beautiful day with which to enjoy their special occasion.

Indeed, as the morning progressed, the sun shone brightly, accompanied by a gentle breeze that was just enough to soften the heat of this gorgeous summer's day. In fact, the whole of creation seemed to be smiling upon Shackellby Downes today.

A small reserve near the church in which the wedding was to be held, was the picturesque venue chosen by the couple for their wedding photographs to be taken. After those had been attended to, they would join with family and friends at the Centre which had been radically transformed for the occasion.

A large marquee had been erected at the side of the building. This was where guests would gather for the wedding reception. When this was over, festivities would continue in a more relaxed manner, inside the Centre itself.

Meanwhile, at the motel in which Eden, Vicky, and Dorothy, were staying, it was all hands to the deck, organizing and making preparations for Eden's big moment. The special dress which was to be revealed for the first time at the ceremony, was checked thoroughly for any creases or marks, and after careful examination, was pronounced fit to wear by a nervous, yet excited Eden.

Various people discreetly came to, and left the motel, as Eden's hair and makeup were attended to.

The townsfolk, in general, were highly anticipating this occasion, with some of the residents with one question uppermost in their minds. Would the prophecy given by Geoff Steadman be fulfilled or not? For many, this was the day of reckoning.

There was a high degree of interest in this wedding.

About an hour before the ceremony was due to begin, people began to flock into the church, eager to secure a prime seat. By 1.40 pm the church was almost filled to capacity.

Mark arrived with his cousin and best man, William. He stood nervously at the front of the church, chatting a little to Mike Brewer who was to marry the couple, as he awaited the arrival of his bride.

Christine Brewer, along with members of Mark's family and several distant relatives of Eden, were seated in the front row. Vicky Morgan's parents were in attendance, as were several long time friends of the young bride. It was Dorothy, who had been given the honour of escorting Eden down the aisle in the absence of both of her parents.

It was expected that Dorothy, Vicky, and Eden would arrive

together. The church was filled with the sound of muffled conversation, as those gathered, eagerly waited to catch a glimpse of the bride. As 2 pm approached, Mark checked his watch, inhaling deeply. Mike Brewer, leaning towards him, reminded him that it was a tradition for the bride to be a little late for her wedding. However, Mark felt ill at ease. He would not be able to settle fully, until the love of his life was safely at his side. He had waited so long to take her as his own.

Mark's anxiety heightened as he glanced at the group of media personnel, who – although barred from the church itself – were gathered just to the side of the doors to the building. Complete with cameras and note pads, they were obviously also awaiting Eden's arrival. Mark shuffled his feet slightly as he wondered what Eden's reaction would be upon seeing them gathered just outside, intruding upon her and Mark's special day.

Finally, at approximately 2.05 pm a small commotion, as well as the sound of cameras snapping outside, announced the arrival of the bride, bringing the entire congregation into an immediate and complete silence.

Mark quietly exhaled in an effort to steady his breathing, as he fixed his eyes firmly upon the entrance to the church.

All in attendance turned their eyes, as one, upon Eden, who stood framed in the doorway with Dorothy at her side and Vicky standing behind her.

Eden stood, poised, glowing with confidence, ready to walk down the aisle to join her husband to be. Her glossy, dark hair, worn loose, cascaded down her back, and a miniature white carnation was fixed in place amongst her curls. Her piercing hazel eyes sparkled with excitement as she stood for a few seconds, savouring the moment.

Eden wore a simple, yet stunning ankle-length, strapless, white silken dress which came in at the waist, displaying her slim figure to perfection. The bodice of this dress was overlaid with white lace.

However, it was not the glamorous dress, or Eden's sparkling eyes, that arrested the gaze of many of the folks gathered in the church that afternoon. Almost everyone stared at Eden's shoulders, neck and upper chest areas, all of which were visible in the lovely wedding gown, in which she was attired.

Audible gasps could be heard from some of those gathered in the church.

Among the gasps were partially stifled whispers, denouncing the prophet, Geoff Steadman, and the words he had spoken over Eden just months earlier at the opening of the stadium. The words 'false prophet' could be heard, muttered by some.

The horrific scarring on Eden's body had not diminished, even a little. It stood out, still glaringly obvious. The crowd stirred as the atmosphere in the church became one of stunned shock.

However, both Eden and Mark were entirely oblivious to the crowd, as Dorothy, taking Eden's arm, began to slowly walk with her down the aisle towards Mark who was waiting beside the altar at the front of the church.

It was as though the eyes of both Eden and Mark, were locked into the gaze of the other.

Eden and Dorothy, with Vicky trailing, walked to where Mark was standing. Mike Brewer stood beside Mark and his best man, ready to marry the beautiful couple.

As the bride finally joined her adoring fiancé, the ceremony began, with vows being exchanged as well as wedding rings.

At the close of the ceremony, Mike pronounced Eden and Mark to be husband and wife.

Tears of love and joy spilled unashamedly from Mark's eyes. Eden also wiped her eyes, although carefully, so as not to disturb her makeup.

This was indeed a deliriously happy couple, who were obviously very much in love. As they exited the church, hand in hand, to the sound of a well known love song being played in the background on the church's piano, neither of the two so much as glanced at the crowd standing respectfully in the church on either side of them.

After everyone had left the church, with the ceremony over, Mike and Christine Brewer remained for a few minutes, in the now empty building, sitting together in silence. Finally, Mike spoke to his wife.

"The words of the prophet certainly came to pass," he commented.

Christine nodded in agreement and replied, "That young lady was definitely healed."

Mike nodded before responding to his wife. "It's a pity that most people missed the miracle," he said.

Christine agreed. "Eden was indeed healed, but not in the way that most people expected. Did you see her confidence? Her joy? Her poise?" she asked Mike.

"Yes," he replied. "Inner healing, the most valuable kind." He continued to speak. "I wonder why, as human beings, we are so often too quick to make judgements based on outward appearances?" Christine shrugged her shoulders and, hand in hand, the pastor and his wife left the building to join in the ongoing festivities of the occasion.

THE END